Light & Dark

A Short Story Collection

Light & Dark

A Short Story Collection

David Mokotoff

First edition published in 2017

ISBN: 978-0-692-03381-4

Disclaimer
These stories are entirely works of fiction. As such, any characters portrayed and names are fictional. Any resemblance to a real person is purely coincidental. Finally, some of the cities and locations are real, while others are fictional.

Cover & Interior Design
Joan Greenblatt
www.CenterPointeMedia.com

Dedication

*This work is dedicated to my beautiful
wife, Denise, who encouraged me to undertake
the craft of short story writing.*

Light & Dark

Table of Contents

Light & Dark

Introduction

People are neither all good nor all bad. Darkness is always followed by light, and even the brightest stars shine more brilliantly upon the black background of deep space. My goal in creating this anthology was two-fold. First, of course, is to entertain, and the other was to make the reader think about the intricacy of human nature. Heroes and heroines are never 100 percent good people, as they always have some flaws. And evil people can often be found to have some redeeming qualities and evoke empathy. Although the stories that follow have no plots that tie one to another, there is a recurring theme of exploring this dichotomy in the characters.

I became interested in short stories following the publication of my memoir, *The Moose's Children: A Memoir of Betrayal, Death and Survival.* A novel seemed too daunting and it was my wife, Denise, who suggested I try short stories. Even at a young age, I had enjoyed the short works of Joyce Carol Oates, Ernest Hemingway, and Edgar Allen Poe. I now found myself reading various anthologies of short prose. Ultra-short stories, or so-called *nano* or *flash fiction*, usually of 300 to 500 words or less, also intrigued me. Thus, you will find three of these included.

The reader will find clear threads of my prior career as a medical doctor running about, as well as my hobbies of fishing and cooking. However, I strove to get out of my comfort zone and write about none of these. Hence, "The Lover of Things and Super Girl," "The Art of Jumping," and "Dog Sense" are outside of those margins.

As I read various short story anthologies, I did find a recurring theme of stories ending ambiguously. This seems to be in vogue and I presume this is to get the reader to imagine an ending, but I find this can also be accomplished within the confines of a tidier story. Sometimes a story will just flow effortlessly and others will nibble at me like termites on wood. I can go days or weeks without writing, although it is easier when I write daily. I like to construct a stereotype and then tear it apart. If the reader feels my plot is predictable, then I feel like I have let him or her down.

I admire those writers whose craft comes easily, like a river flowing downhill. For me it is a labor of love. It takes very thick skin to write and invite potential rejection and ridicule more often than praise or success. It is not for the timid, weak, or insecure. For me, the burning desire to write is always present, no matter if two, or 2,000 people, will be reading my work product. For someone who has spent most of his life utilizing only the left (rational) side of his brain, this exploration into the right (creative) side is challenging and refreshing. A friend explained that personal growth only comes about by doing "not doings." That is, forcing one's self to do things that we by our nature and mind find difficult, repugnant, or uncomfortable. I have found that a useful guide. Without exploring beyond our usual habits and choices, we can learn nothing and end up with a boring and predictable life. It may be safe; however, it is also dull and unexciting. For many, sameness and repetition is enough. For me, that means not exploring the wonders of life. I hope readers of *Light and Dark* will come away feeling they have found something that questions their assumptions and values and provides diversion in the process.

Light & Dark

Light

The only thing he could see was black—not a color, but the absence of all light. They had lied to him. He remembered all the stories of near-death victims who saw a tunnel with brilliant white light at the end. He was neither cold nor hot. Everything was just dark. He could see—no feel—himself hovering over a body in a hospital bed. His last memory before that was of sudden, searing pain in the back of his head, and then nothing. He felt weightless and loved the sensation of floating. There was no up or down or right or left. He could not sense a beginning or end of his space. Not only could he not see, but also he could not hear or smell. He could not touch his environment either. It was not soft or dry, rough or smooth. His only knowledge was that, on some level, he was aware that he was present, but he knew not where.

His wife, Clara, stood over the bed as she watched multiple tubes entering and exiting her husband Paul's body. The ventilator breathed in and out in a well-syncopated rhythm. The heartbeat blips on the electrical screen kept time like a metronome. Other RGB colors on the black screen kept detailed recordings of his pulse, breathing rate, blood pressure, and oxygen saturation level.

His doctor entered the room, and she immediately rose from the reclining chair to meet him.

"Anything new?" she asked.

He shook his head, "No, I'm afraid not."

"How long can he go on like this?"

The doctor thought for a moment, and then answered slowly, "Days, weeks, months ... not years."

He could see the pain on her well-made face, surgically corrected to look younger than her six decades of life. Her pearl earrings matched her necklace, and her black dress fit her well-trimmed body, its color raising the specter of an imminent funeral.

"We will do another EEG and CAT scan today to see if there has been any change," he said.

"But there are still no plans for surgery, right?"

"No. But these tests will help with prognosis and"—he wanted to put this delicately—"end of life decisions. Does he having a living will?"

Biting her lip, she answered right away. "Yes. I'll bring it in if you would like a copy."

"Yes, please."

He listened to his patient's heart and lungs in a cursory manner, noted the numbers on the screen, and then tapped an electronic note into the bedside desktop computer before leaving. As he reached for the door, he turned to her and said, "I'm sorry."

For Clara, life was divided into two distinct time periods—before and after the incident. He had sustained a subarachnoid hemorrhage, or bleeding into his brain. Medical words like *aneurysm*, *mid-line shift*, and *intra-cerebral* washed over her like cold waves. Their meaning was poorly defined but the gravity of their implications was clear, and none of it was good.

"What are his chances?" she asked the first day in the intensive care unit.

"1 out of 10, at best," the doctor had said. "But we'll have to wait and see; these things can be unpredictable."

Over the next three days, she reflected on their thirty years of marriage. Some of it, of course, was wonderful: three beautiful children, a gorgeous home, plenty of money, and a mostly faithful husband. A neurosurgeon by trade, it was a cruel irony that his life should hang in the balance by a disease he had seen and treated many times.

A prior dinner conversation kept surfacing in her mind.

"If I'm ever alive only because of machines, don't hesitate to take me off."

She would always say, "Oh don't worry, that will never happen."

"Clara," he retorted, "I'm a doctor and I see this all the time. Just say you'll pull the plug." In reality, his latest episode of philandering was probably stirring the guilt part of his consciousness, worrying that God or karma would punish him for his infidelity.

"Paul, I don't want to ..."

"Just say it, damn it."

She then placed her glass of chardonnay on a linen doily and looked up, but averted direct eye contact.

"Yes. I will. But only if it seems beyond hope."

"Hope is a subjective phrase. Rely on the doctors. Just make sure it's not some goddamn 'save the world' idealistic intern or resident. Okay?"

"Okay."

Time had no meaning in his current condition. He could have been in this state for one hour, one day, or one year. There was no pain either. He could, however, now hear voices nearby. But he did not know if it was his family. They were familiar, in some sense, but he could not identify names. He felt neither sadness nor joy; he was devoid of any emotion. He was just present, in some form. He had only one wish: to see some light. On one level, he knew that he was—or had been— a doctor, a surgeon perhaps. Other than, that he could recall nothing.

It was Day Four after his bleed. Three children arrived from out of town, camping at their father's bedside, holding hands and exchanging desperate hugs. Evelyn was the oldest. She was like a sturdy hand on the steering wheel—steady and pragmatic. She had not yet married, instead choosing an executive career at a forensic accounting firm. Then there were the twins, Candice and Alexander. Candice (Candy) was the wild child. She flew from one job to the next and had a long string of ex-boyfriends. She was quick to please and even quicker to anger. Alexander was the good boy who went to medical school and married young. Although he and his wife had no children yet, he was the most emotional and fearful member of the trio.

Exiting the room, they had phones glued to their ears, giving friends and other family members updates. Nothing had changed. They became familiar with the hospital routine—change of nursing shift at 7 AM, then a parade of medical students, interns, residents, and neurology fellows. Then a hospital specialist, or hospitalist, and finally the neurologist would pass through. The last doctor seemed to be calling the shots, but he had a heavy accent and was a bit hard to understand. Clara found herself leaning into his face, as if this might improve his English. His name was Dr. Patel, or was it Desai or Shah? She could never remember. *These Indians always seemed to have the same damn names*, she thought.

On the afternoon of the fourth day, the neurologist had a subtle smile. Clara and the children stood up immediately, hungry for any tidbit of good news. They doted on every spoken word and would read optimism into even a head tilt.

"The size of the bleed has stabilized," he began. "It may be a tiny bit smaller, and there is less pressure on his brain. His EEG is also showing a bit more organized cortical activity."

"What does all that mean?" asked Clara.

"It means we may be on the road to recovery here, but I must warn you that there are no guarantees of a return to full mental capacity. And he could take a turn for the worse at any time." The family did not hear the second part of the sentence, only the first.

The children heaved sighs of relief, and the two daughters began to cry. Andrew said, "Well, I guess that's as best as we can expect now."

"Yes," said the doctor. "We will continue to feed him intravenously until his stomach starts to work, and attempt to wean him off of the ventilator. But again, please keep your expectations low—these are very delicate and unpredictable cases, and anything can happen."

The children nodded their heads, and Clara reached out for the doctor's deep brown hand. He covered it with his other hand in a sympathetic gesture, but Clara noticed that his hands were cool and his grip, soft. *Probably just cultural*, she thought. After he left, she collapsed into the reclining chair as the children surrounded and hugged her. She was physically and emotionally spent.

The children returned several hours later with styrofoam boxes of take-out Thai food. Clara poked at her chicken pad thai, while Candy munched noisily on her spring rolls. Evelyn spoke first.

"Mom, does Dad have a living will?"

Clara shook her head.

"Why not?"

"Because he didn't want one. However, he did tell me that if he were ever to be at the point where only machines kept him alive, to 'pull the plug.' "

"But we're not there yet are we?" asked Alex.

No one wanted to answer.

The children knew their father had a lot of money, but had no idea how he would provide for them in his will. As was typical of many doctors, he chose to deny rather than deal with the reality of death. In actuality, all of his estate would fall to Clara for tax purposes upon his death, and the children's inheritance would have to wait until after she passed. In addition to death, money was another subject rarely discussed by the family. The children learned that they needed to be independent as soon as they graduated from college or grad school. However, prior to that, Paul had provided for all of their tuition and living expenses. Evelyn and Alex were grateful. Candy, on the other hand, could not understand why the gravy train could not continue and was resentful.

Everything was no longer black—it had turned gray. There certainly were no colors, and he couldn't, at first, make out faces or figures. But he started to see forms in the shadows.

They moved slowly around him and he perceived a return of some of his senses. First was smell…familiar…alcohol, and at times, body fluids. Then noises began to abound—a dropped bottle, loud music, and conversations with words he did not recognize. Again, he had no sense of the passing of time. Next he noticed that he was cold, then hot. He thought a voice said something like, "fever…temperature spike…septic…antibiotics…" but again, they had no meaning or definition. Finally came an awareness: that is me in the bed and I am deathly ill.

A feeding tube was inserted into his stomach on Day Five. Multiple doctors said his central venous catheter, or tube, that was giving him medicine and calories, had to be removed, as it had become infected. Stronger antibiotics would be given and a new line placed. Dr. Patel arrived with another glimmer of hope. The family was told in advance to assemble.

"I have been speaking with some other physicians, and we feel that since there has been some improvement, we might want to address the issue of what caused his bleed," he said slowly, letting them digest the information in small servings. "We did an MRI yesterday and there appears to be an aneurysm inside the brain. It hasn't burst yet but is slowly leaking. That is what caused his bleeding and his stroke."

Before he could continue Clara burst out, "STROKE? No one ever said he had a stroke! When did that happen?"

Dr. Patel looked perplexed and caught off guard.

"I'm sorry. I thought someone explained to you that a bleed

inside the brain causes damage to the brain tissue, in other words a stroke. Just different than the usual forms."

Clara shuffled her feet a bit as the children searched her eyes for verification.

"I don't recall. Perhaps someone did. Does that change anything?"

"No. Anyway, operating at this time is far too risky, but with advances in our catheter technology we may be able to fix it less invasively."

"Go on," she said.

"Well, we have specialized radiologists, x-ray doctors, and some experimental techniques where they can thread a catheter through the artery in his groin up to the artery in his brain and close off the leaking blood vessel. The success rate is about sixty to seventy-five percent."

"Any if we don't?" Clara asked.

"In my opinion, it is unlikely he will ever make a full recovery and the artery can leak more or burst at any time in the future. On the other hand, there are cases where the artery seals itself off without further bleeding. I know this is a terribly hard decision for all of you to make."

"When do we need to make it?" she asked.

"As long as he is stable or improving, a few days perhaps, but certainly not today. We need to see some continued improvement first. I just wanted you to know all of the options."

"Thank you," she said. "We will talk about it more."

She sensed the children's desire to talk.

"Mom, we need to have a game plan here," started Evelyn.

"Not today. I just can't yet."

The twins looked on in silence.

Shadows slowly became more defined. He began to recognize arms, legs, torsos, and a head. He could not make out faces, however. Sounds became more frequent and familiar. He heard beeping on a monitor. He also became aware of a constant vertigo or dizziness. It was not unpleasant, but it was omnipresent and profound. He noted his throat was sore and his mouth was dry. A picture, from his memory, of many patients who were on ventilators, or breathing machines, with tubes down their throats, slowly emerged. He could sense someone, or something, turning him on his side in the bed, and applying a warm, wet cloth to his skin. An ill-defined heaviness in the room began to lighten, and he heard voices that seemed familiar. There was a gentle pat on his skin. Was it his arm? He became aware of his legs, but he could not move them. He wanted to speak or scream, but nothing came out of his mouth.

By Day Seven, the process of weaning him off the ventilator had begun, and his nurses and doctors took note of more stable breathing, blood pressure, and heart rate. His infection seemed to be under control. The neurologist remained upbeat and "cautiously optimistic." Lord, how Clara hated that cliché. It meant nothing and was contradictory. Its only purpose was for the doctor to hedge his bets on his patient's survival.

Evelyn and Alex had scoured the internet in search of answers and advice for the bleeding artery closure procedure called a coil embolization. They found no consensus. Evelyn was in favor and Alex was opposed. Candy deferred and would not voice an opinion, saying only, "I don't know anything about any of this." Clara became increasingly agitated.

"I appreciate your input, but ultimately, this is my decision to make," Clara told them. "Your father wouldn't want to live this way, I'm sure. He was always a risk-taker. Not reckless, mind you, but I just feel he would take any chance to beat this. Besides, I can't live with this hanging over us forever."

They would ultimately defer to her. On Day Eight, late in the morning, she would see a finger move, ever so slightly. She glimpsed life in his eyes and made her decision to proceed. A neuroradiologist came to speak with the family and, without hesitation, she signed the lengthy consent form, much of which she did not want to read. As a family, they had never been religious, but she decided to pray.

Finally, he could make out faces, and saw his legs and toes as he looked down. An impulse traveled from the left side of his brain to his right hand, and he lifted his index finger. Someone grabbed his hand, and he felt warmth on his cheek—they were tears, but the tears were not his—they were from the woman standing over him. Clara, his wife. His eyes roved slowly from side to side and he recognized his children. He saw Alex and

Candy weeping. Through his vertiginous fog, he felt scared. Why was he here? What had happened to him? His short-term memory was gone.

On Day Ten, he was taken to the Radiology suite, where his groin was prepped and draped after being washed with iodine soap. He could feel a pinprick in his right groin area and then mild pressure. He heard music in the background, a beautiful voice singing Ava Maria. Then he felt a grenade explode in his head. The searing pain was overwhelming.

"Shit," the radiologist said. "The guide wire just perforated the artery. I need a stent stat," he barked to his assistants.

"What about the coil procedure?"

"No time for that now. We've got a real problem here."

As the doctor squirted colorless x-ray contrast through the tube, the scope of the problem manifested itself. Instead of staying inside the artery, it had spilled out into the surrounding tissue, indicative of a critical tear and bleed. They worked for almost an hour but could not save him.

Clara sobbed into the arms of Alex and Candy. Even Evelyn, always stoical, broke down and wailed. Alex had the urge to say, "I told you so," or "he'd still be alive if you had listened to me." However, Evelyn sensed his rage and before he could speak, she shut him off with a stern, "Not now, Alex. Please."

There was no tunnel. However, there was brilliant, warm white light, and it was everywhere. Paul no longer had pain or dizziness. He wasn't scared; in fact, he was strangely calm. He looked down at his body, detached from any awareness of it being his, and watched as a bevy of people in white coats pushed on his chest and applied electrical paddles to restart his heart. He felt weightless and buoyant. As he floated higher and higher, the image of his body faded but the comfortable, beautiful light bathed him from inside to out. He felt peace and serenity.

Light & Dark

Deadlyfoods.com

My name is Danny, and I am a writer. Because of my writing career I almost died—several times. There are more dangerous jobs in the world than writing a food blog, like policeman, firefighter, or commercial fisherman. However, I didn't write just any blog. No, I took it to the extreme. "Deadly Foods" was the name of my blog. I would travel and taste exotic foods, flirting with illness and death on multiple occasions. How I came upon this career choice is a good story by itself. But you may not be interested in that. One thing I have learned from this experience, however, is sometimes you can't undo what has been done.

Read and write. Write and read. Time and again I heard these dictums preached as a way to improve my writing. But the more I read, the more discouraged I got. I would devour novels and other books daily and admire the ease with which the author could paint the details of a scene, a face, a body, clothes, or even the air. Yet when I sat down to write, all I got was plain vanilla. Or at least that's what my teachers said. But I fell in love with the feel and the sound of words. The thesaurus became my best friend. So how could someone with mediocre writing skills and no particular career have become so successful? The answer is serendipity. See? There I go again. I could have just said luck but serendipity sounds slick and sexy.

I faked my way through high school. My grades were okay to good, but it was my SAT scores that got me into a great college—MIT. Yes, that great engineering school in Cambridge, Massachusetts. Most people don't know this, but it pumps out more than just brilliant engineers. It has a great creative writing school. Who knew? I didn't. I was a natural test taker. I had an uncanny knack for predicting what the test maker was asking. My math scores were very good, but my writing scores were a perfect 800. Imagine my shock when I soon learned in college that such flawlessness did not automatically translate into superb creative writing skills.

"Mr. English." Yes, I know that's a funny name for an aspiring writer but hey, I didn't pick it. "Just because your SAT scores were high does not mean you are guaranteed a successful writing career," said Mr. Hamilton, my freshman English teacher and future writing coach. He assured me I could get a career translating unreadable engineering and technical manuals into plain English, but what's the fun in that? My dream of becoming a famous author, he discouraged.

"Thousands will try, but few will succeed," he would say to me. "Despite what the managers of writing courses and re-treats might tell you, creative writing is not something you can learn—it is something the right side of your brain is born with." That was a depressing thought and I discounted it, wondering: *How much can this guy know about writing if he always ends a sentence with a preposition?*

It was at the end of my junior year when the idea for ex-treme foods was born. I always liked to eat and cook. In fact, I had contemplated going to chef school but that seemed like too much work. Anyway, some friends and I decided to rent a cottage on Cape Cod for a few weeks that summer. While dining out one night in Wellfleet, and after one too many Sam-uel Adams lagers, we decided to have an oyster-eating contest. How many could you down in 10 minutes? The six of us kicked in $20, (above and beyond the cost of the shellfish), and the winner took the pool.

I was the last man standing at four dozen of the gooey bivalves and stood up to a small crowd cheering me. With both hands raised into the air, I barely noticed that my five compet-itors were now long gone, all evacuating their stomachs in the bathroom. Their gastrointestinal distress lasted long into the evening and early morning hours. Our cottage smelled like a sewer treatment plant and I finally resorted to sleeping on the porch hammock.

Sipping a cup of coffee the following morning, the green-around-the-gills crew began to appear. Pale and sweaty, the spent boys gawked at the placement of anything into my mouth. Tom Sweet, a shy engineering student from Montpelier, Vermont said, "Dude, I can't believe you didn't get sick. There is something wrong with you. No, seriously—you are like an eating machine. You should go into competitive eating or something."

"You mean like taking on Joey Chestnut at the Nathan's Fourth of July Hot Dog eating contest at Coney Island?"

"Yeah, something like that."

"Nah."

"Why not?"

"Simple." I smiled. "I don't like hot dogs."

But his suggestion got me thinking. After a quick internet search I could not find a blogger who excelled at eating deadly foods—not bizarre foods; heck anyone can down grasshoppers, bugs, and mountain oysters. I meant near-death experience stuff. Now this could be a real headline and money grabber, not to mention a turn-on for chicks—well, maybe not. I liked to write and eat. I had a cast iron stomach and hadn't got sick since I was on a whale watching tour out of Provincetown when I was twelve. The more I thought about it, the more excited I became. I could market this puppy and maybe even grab a reality show spot on the Discovery Channel.

So I pulled out my laptop and entered "deadly foods" into Google. There were the usual suspects like puffer fish, ackee fruit, wild mushrooms, and then some surprises like leaves of rhubarb. The challenge was to flirt with death, but not actually die. So I would start small and low risk and work my way up.

"Hey Teddy, this is Danny. I need your help with a webpage. How much would you charge?" Teddy Granger was a self-admitted tech addict and geek extraordinaire. He still owed me from being on the losing side of the oyster bet.

"For you bro, a discount. But what's it about?"

After giving him my thirty-second pitch summary, there was silence at the other end of the phone.

"Seriously? I always knew you were a bit off but this shit seems a bit gnarly." (Translation: you are whacked.)

I told him the focus would be a weekly blog with some pictures and or video, a short bio, and a place for comments.

"That's too easy," he said, "How about $200?"

"Deal."

I found Carl Spinner online. He was a budding chef in Vermont who hunted his own food in the wild. When I told him I was an investigative reporter working on finding local and sustainable foods (good buzz word), he invited me to visit his farm and kitchen.

His farm was located about 50 miles northeast of the college town Bennington, nestled inside of the Green Mountains National Park. It was a few miles off Highway 7, with good signage pointing to its remote wooded location. The name of the farm and restaurant was intriguing: "The Feral Fungus." The barn was a weathered gray and brown clapboard. Cows, hens, chickens, and pigs wandered around a fenced area clucking and grunting. Although it was early September, it was cold and humid when I arrived and the air smelled like a mixture of pine and must. Carl greeted me in Duluth overalls and calf-high black rubber boots. He was six foot five, lanky, with long hair and a graying beard. He appeared to have stepped out of the set of "Duck Dynasty," except his politics were left of center. His firm handshake almost crushed my metacarpals.

"Ready to go hunting?" he said. "It's been rainy this summer so the mushrooms have been plentiful and easy to find."

I nodded but felt strangely out of place in my Levi jeans, New Balance running shoes, and J. Crew sweater vest. He grabbed two bamboo baskets and handed me one as we set off into the woods.

"So how did you get interested in wild mushrooms?" I asked.

"I always liked them. Then went to chef school after dropping out of college. I inherited this farm from my dad who died a few years back in a hunting accident."

"I'm sorry for your loss," I said.

"Thanks," he replied, but by his silence, I could tell he didn't want to elaborate further.

No more than a couple hundred yards into the woods, he held up his right hand, signaling me to stop.

"There they are," he said, pointing to an orange-red outcropping by a rock under a tall pine.

"Lobster mushrooms," he said, bending over to pluck one. He held it under my nose and not only was it lobster colored, but it had a faint seafood scent. We picked some and moved on. As my feet crunched on some fallen pine needles, Carl stared at my feet as if he just saw either a python or a bar of gold, and said, "Whoa."

"Whoa what?" I asked.

"Look down. What do you see?"

"Uh, pines needles and some oak leaves?"

"Yes, and…?"

My silence revealed my ignorance but he smiled and said happily, "A prize—black trumpet mushrooms! They are really flavorful." He quickly dug up a handful and tossed them into the baskets.

The next find was mine and more obvious.

"What about these?" I asked extending my hand towards a clump of grayish-white clamshell-shaped fungus growing off the base of a pine tree.

"Those are oysters and will work too. They are more bland and ordinary, but I mix them in with others when I make my mushroom risotto or bisque."

We only picked half the crop because Carl adhered to a strict sustainability policy.

Further along, I spotted a lovely red species pushing up from the ground.

"How about these?"

"Ah … those are Russula emetica. They are also known as the vomiting Russula," he said dryly. From the description I got the gist.

"Can they kill you?" I asked.

"Rarely," he said, "But you'll have projectiles coming out of both ends for a few hours if you eat 'em."

"Are there ones that are more dangerous?"

"Amanita bisporigera, aka, the destroying angel, which causes liver and kidney failure."

"So how do you tell them apart?" I asked. He looked at me quizzically. "I mean the edible from the poisonous ones?"

"Experience and strict adherence to identification. The bottom line is, if you're not sure, then don't harvest it."

"Any other warning signs?"

"To be sure you have the right mushroom, place the cap on a piece of white paper and let it drop its spores. Different varieties will have different-colored spores, which will help you identify them. If the spore color is blue, that could be bad." I gradually understood that for him, the spectrum for "bad" ranged between rank-tasting and lethal.

As Carl walked on, I quickly reached down and plucked a couple of the forbidden red guys and threw them into my basket.

An hour or so later we were done. Carl invited me back to the kitchen but I said I had a long ride back home. I thanked him, scribbled some notes on a fake reporter's pad and took off.

Sitting in my den, I stared at the Russula mushrooms. I did an internet search and convinced myself if I ate them at least I wouldn't die. So I began to pound out a blog post and mounted my iPhone on a tripod. I clicked on my Periscope app, figuring if I were going to die at least it would be recorded online for the world to see. What can I say? I'm a millennial and was raised with devices in my hand before I could read or write. If I were going to check out, at least my last testament would be recorded for other socially conscious geeks to witness.

I checked the phone's battery and started recording.

"So I'm going to stir-fry these bad boys in a little bit of butter and olive oil." I sliced them thin and threw them into the hot pan. After dumping them out on a paper towel, I grabbed a tall glass of water and a cold Cigar City beer. I downed a bit of each one, raised my glass to the camera, smiled broadly, and said, "Cheers."

The stinging on my tongue and lips was instantaneous. I felt like I had swallowed a handful of wasps.

I slammed the beer and tried to smile up at the phone.

"Well, that was nasty," I said. "I don't think I ate enough of them to get sick. The taste is so putrid I doubt you can eat enough of these to get really ill. In fact ..."

In fact, I couldn't finish my sentence, because saliva started to pour into my mouth like a burst dam. I reached for a nearby wastebasket and started to puke up what little lunch I had ingested a few hours earlier.

Between hurls, I tried to smile.

"If I collapse and stop breathing, can someone call 911 please?"

I realized how ridiculous this must have sounded. No one

out there watching this sick performance knew where I lived, and even if they did, by the time the ambulance arrived, I would be assuming room temperature.

Fortunately, after about twenty more minutes of retching, the sweating and shaking start to ease.

"And that, my friends, is why you should never forage for mushrooms without an expert to identify your harvest. Until next time, I remain the ever-inquisitive 'Dangerous Foods Blogger.'"

The name had just popped into my head and seemed to fit.

The response was instantaneous and epic. My email, Twitter, and Facebook accounts were blowing up. I had over a thousand hits on YouTube. There were, of course, a few observers who were sure I was mentally ill and should seek professional help. However, most were willing lovers of the macabre.

"Dude, you need to start a reality show; seriously, that was awesome!"

Others were a little less enthusiastic but still supportive.

"Mr. English. Your dangerous food video blog was incredible. It was like *Bizarre Foods with Andrew Zimmern* on steroids."

One email came from the mushroom hunter Carl himself, who only said, "Do you have a death wish?"

The more I read, the more I became convinced that I had really tapped into something huge. Sure, it was sick and prurient, but I thought, *Hell, I could be famous.* That is, if I lived.

The trick was to thread the needle between just being sick

and being dead. *No problem*, my mind said. I would read everything I could find about the toxic eats and stay on the upright side of living. Where others had failed, I would succeed. But how to follow this one with a more thrilling second act would take some thought.

It took a few days, however, after I purged my body of the last traces of the noxious fungus, I moved onto fish—puffer fish, that is. *Fugu* is the Japanese word for puffer fish—genus Takifugu, Lagocephalus, or Sphoeroides. Fugu can be lethally poisonous due to its tetrodotoxin; therefore, it must be carefully prepared to remove toxic parts and to avoid contaminating the meat. In fact, in Japan national law controls its preparation and only chefs with several years of experience are allowed to serve it. Accidental deaths have been reported and are not uncommon. The liver is the tastiest part but also the most concentrated with poison. When the fillets are cleaned properly, it is usually served as sushi or sashimi.

I did not know much about this toxin but after doing some research, even I was a bit frightened. As a neurotoxin it paralyzes muscles, including the diaphragm, so you can't breathe. It is similar to the poison used in sarin gas and is 1,200 times deadlier than cyanide. But here's the kicker: you're still awake. So essentially you asphyxiate and are totally awake as it is happening. This was definitely not my idea of a good way to die, online or otherwise.

The best way to do this, if I was stupid enough to do it, would be a trip to Japan where I could sample the stuff from an expert chef. As my student budget would not allow it, I crossed that off my list. With the aid of the world wide web, I found a chef in the Back Bay part of Boston who was a trained fugu chef. I stopped in late one afternoon as he was prepping sushi and sashimi and introduced myself. I dared not tell him my website's name or my intention. Instead, I lied and said I was working on a food blog of interesting and potentially lethal food. Yoshi was his name. He looked to be about forty years old with jet-black hair, but age is tough to estimate in Asians. He had a well-starched white shirt and apron and clogs on his feet. Fortunately for me, his English was limited but he nodded his head and spoke the universally understood word, "Okay."

It was not yet 5:00, so business was slack. Two other young male sushi chefs were busy assembling spider rolls, fresh eel, and hamachi. Yoshi reached behind to the cooler and pulled out an ugly brownish fish that from my online study I knew was a puffer. He showed me how to skin and clean it properly as I snapped pictures with my phone. He used an ultrathin knife and made slender translucent slices. He took extreme care to avoid the skin and internal organs, especially the liver. I asked him if I could try and his black, bushy eyebrows raised up and a crooked smile turned downward. He grunted, shook his head no, and handed me another fish. He tossed me latex gloves that needed to be changed after handling the poisonous parts.

As I scraped the skin away from the fillet, Yoshi folded his arms and frowned. He took over and tried to salvage the butchering I had started. Then I grabbed the intestines and liver and started to throw them out as he had shown me. I paused, looking at the liver and dangled it over my mouth. The humorless chef began to scream and curse in Japanese. He pointed a finger to the exit and demanded I leave. I made a hasty retreat to the door as he picked up a ginza knife and began to wave it like a Samurai sword. With all the hysteria and commotion, he didn't notice me slipping the small, brown organ into my pocket.

Back at my apartment, I called friends and started to set up another live video feed. This new attempt at self-destruction actually scared me a bit. In fact, when I told Teddy about it, he insisted that he attend before I pulled off my latest gastronomical stunt.

While waiting for him to come over, I ran out and got some sushi rolls. California rolls, with no poisonous parts at all. By the time I was back, Teddy had arrived with a six-pack of Pabst Blue Ribbon.

"Is that for you or me?" I asked.

Cracking a sideways smile, he answered, "Me, and the EMS guys after they get here."

I groaned and guzzled a beer. As Teddy helped me set up the video feed, I put on a black T-shirt, figuring if I was going to puke, it wouldn't be too revolting on a dark background. Teddy gave me a thumbs up and I started my next 15 minutes of fame.

"Danny English here with deadlyfoods.com. Today, I am showing you what not to eat next time you're in the mood for raw fish. No, not these California rolls here. Look over here." I held up my tiny sliver of liver to the camera.

"Looks innocent enough, doesn't it? Well, this tiny liver is from a puffer fish." I cut to a web image of the whole fish. "Their meat is edible but the eyes, intestines, and organs can be lethal. The toxin in here is similar to what the South American Indians put in their poison darts. It is a neurotoxin, and it can stop your breathing but not your brain. So you remain alert as you suffocate to death. But I'm only going to try a tiny piece. I have a friend here just in case." I flipped the camera phone around and said, "Wave to world, Teddy!"

Teddy held up his beer for a kind of high five, and then I flipped the camera back.

"Well, here we go." I picked up a sushi roll, dipped it in soy sauce, and stabbed some wasabi and pickled ginger with chopsticks and downed it. I then took a swallow of beer. I repeated the action with another roll, but this time took some tweezers and teased away a piece of liver about the size of a raisin. I dropped it on top.

"Well, if I die, I want to say Mom and Dad, I love you. And Sally, my dear sister, I'm sorry for how much I teased you." I dangled the item over my mouth and then put it back down. "And oh, Diana, my ex-girlfriend, I still love you."

I gulped the roll and slice of liver down and took another swallow of beer. As I waited for something to happen, I gave a brief lowdown of lethal fish and my encounter with the local sushi chef.

After about fifteen minutes, I said, "Well, it looks like puffer fish liver may not be so deadly after all, at least in small quantities."

Then I started to notice a tingling in my throat and lips and hands. I became short of breath. I described what I was feeling to the camera and turned to Teddy.

"Uh, I think it may be time to call 911."

That was the last thing I remembered for the next two days. Well, actually that wasn't true. I remembered gasping for air and a guy shoving a breathing tube down my throat. It felt like a lead pipe. I couldn't scream. My body was on fire and everything was tingly, but not in good way. I vaguely remember the bumpy ride in the ambulance to the hospital and that was when they shot me full of Propofol (the powerful sedative made famous by Michael Jackson). Then I remembered nothing.

"Danny, Danny. Can you hear me?" I nodded my head. Some young Indian guy in a white lab coat was leaning over me. I knew I was awake because his breath smelled like curry. My eyes fixed on a dark red spot on his lapel and I thought of blood. Then my mind started to work. No, not blood. It looked like beef vindaloo.

"We're going to pull out your breathing tube now. You will be gagging but if you relax you'll be able to breathe."

I felt like a chicken bone was tumbling through my throat. I coughed spasmodically and finally was able to breathe. I couldn't speak much and my throat was sore. I looked around and there were tubes everywhere—tubes in my nose, my elbow, my wrist, and even my dick.

Finally I was able to speak in a subdued and hoarse voice. "Where am I?"

"County hospital, ICU," curry doctor said.

"Did I die?"

"No. But you came very close. If your friend wasn't with you and if EMS hadn't arrived when they did, you would probably be gone."

My mind chewed on that for a bit.

"Would you like to see your family now?"

I nodded my head and he stepped outside of the bleach-smelling room with all of its strange lights and beeping noises. I felt like I was on the Starship Enterprise but Scotty and Captain Kirk were nowhere to be found.

My parents and my sister entered the room. My mother had tears in her eyes. My dad tried to look sympathetic but was just pissed off.

My mom and sister both hugged me.

"Oh Danny, we were so worried about you. Please don't ever do this again."

My dad was less empathetic. He had his arms folded over his chest and just shook his head. "Did you learn this in college?"

"Oh Henry, please not now!" Mom admonished him.

Diana didn't visit or call. I later discovered a text message on my phone from her that said, "You are such an asshole."

I was discharged home two days later and admonished by the medical staff to re-examine my career choice. Upon returning to my apartment and checking my email, I saw that my account had again exploded. My inbox was stuffed. Apart from the usual accolades from the deranged followers of my blog, there were several interview offers from various reality channels, like Travel, Discover, Nat Geo, Lifetime, and Bravo. Some implied that I could easily make a six-figure income with my concept—if I survived.

Again, caution took a back seat to my mind and reason. I figured my mistake had been in not choosing my foods carefully enough. I could handle getting sick but flirting with actual death would be a career killer, so to speak. So I again did an internet search of harmful foods. I quickly eliminated further mushrooms or poisonous fish. The list I found was impressive. The most fascinating was a baby octopus from Japan which continued to move even after being chopped up and cooked, so the consumer might feel tiny suction cups climbing up their throats. Or there was a rare shark from Greenland with no bladder or kidneys so it essentially eliminates toxins by peeing through its skin. Often described as the worst tasting food on earth, it has to be specially prepared and hung up to dry for six months.

As I did my research, offers for live television reality shows poured in. All wanted exclusive contracts with rights to cancel at any time. They would retain control of filming and dangerous food choices. I would be given a small stipend and royalty each time the episode was replayed. There was a strong liability release for injury and death and hold-harmless clause so even my family could not sue in the future. My brain was spinning and I needed some air. It was a beautiful New England fall day with cool, crisp winds and the scent of falling leaves.

I was at a crossroads and felt there was no turning back. I could quit now, while still alive and healthy. Or I could continue on as a well-paid carnival clown. I wandered down to Back Bay, gazing at the old brownstone homes and sailboats on the Charles River. I had so many emails and text messages flying in that I finally turned off my phone just to be able to think. I sat down on a bench and stared out at the water.

A young woman with a bouncing ponytail ran by with her golden doodle. They were engaged in a game of catch. As she launched a dirty saliva-filled tennis ball from a Chuckit launcher, the hairy animal collided into my legs.

"Oh, I'm so sorry. Albert gets distracted when we are playing," she said.

"Albert?" I asked.

"Yes, Albert. My dog."

"Oh yes," I mumbled, having been deep in thought.

She was athletic but not too thin. She wore little-to-no makeup and a Boston Red Sox ball cap. Still in a fog, I had forgotten common courtesy so she took the initiative.

"Sam," she said. "Sam Gardner."

I glanced at her hazel eyes and said, "Sam as in Samantha?"

"No, Sam as in Samuel." She waited for me to laugh but again I was too fogged in to be thinking clearly. Then I remembered one of my doctors had said the prolonged intubation and sedation medications could hang with me for days and even weeks. I started to feel as if I was stoned. I must have been staring blankly and she could see I was not firing with all cylinders.

"Yes, Samantha, of course." She extended her gloved hand and asked, "And you are?"

"Oh. Danny. Danny English." We shook firmly.

Her grip lasted a bit long. A twinkle came to her eye.

"Hey, do I know you? You look familiar. Movie star? TV?"

I hung my head in embarrassment as I released her hand. Not wanting to appear a complete fool, I lied.

"No, I don't think so."

She giggled and then pointed a long finger at me. 'Whoa, wait a minute. You're that deadly foods guy who almost died."

I looked past her gaze and hung my head lower. I picked it up and cracked a half smile, half-smirk.

"Guilty," I said.

Her skin was dark and her eyes almond-shaped. I was certain she was part Asian but figured I would ask her later.

"So I am in the presence of a celebrity."

I blushed. "Well, not yet but maybe on my way."

Neither of us spoke but I could feel some magnet keeping us in a small space, only a few feet apart.

Finally, I spoke. "Would you like to grab a coffee or drink somewhere?"

She did not hesitate. "I would love to but I have to get Albert back home. But maybe a rain check?"

"Sure."

We exchanged phone numbers, shook hands and after patting Albert's curly soft head, I left.

At home I showered and was about to respond to my emails and offers, when my cell phone rang.

"Hey, Danny, it's Sam. I know this is kind of forward of me, but I have the day off from work tomorrow. How about I cook you some dinner?"

"Great. I'll bring some wine. What time?"

"Seven."

"Okay. Wait a minute. What is your address?"

She gave me a street address and apartment number. I entered it into my phone's contact list and thought about how great my life was going. Then I went back to my endless pile of emails and text messages looking for a lucrative TV gig and contract. The one from Nat Geo seemed the most lucrative. I responded and a meeting was set up in three days.

Shortly before seven I arrived at her brownstone apartment and rang her bell. I could hear a dog barking as I was buzzed inside. Sam greeted me at the door with a firm handshake and body language which I read as "It's too early for a kiss." I handed her the bottle of wine as she let me in and I looked around. The interior design was eclectic, part oriental and part IKEA.

There was New Age Enya-like stuff on her stereo and she poured some wine and served crackers and cheese. She slipped off her sandals, which reduced her height to about 5'8", two inches shorter than me. She had a V-neck sweater that plunged down, showing a couple inches of cleavage. Her loose skirt wrapped lazily around her hips. After some small talk I asked, "Since you know what I do, what about you?"

"Law," was her clipped and nondescript answer. Suddenly she rose.

"Oh, I forgot something. I will be right back." She quickly returned with a plate of what appeared to be hummus. What I failed to notice, because my eyes were more focused on her chest, was that the plate was divided into two sections. She scooped up a mouthful on a cracker and handed it to me as she took one from the other side.

"It's a special family recipe, " she said before I asked.

"What's in it?" I asked.

"It's a secret." She grinned and then waited a moment as I stared at her.

"Oh, come on now. You're not going to tell me the host of Deadly Foods is scared of a homemade dip!" She laughed.

Her eyes twinkled as her shoulder-length hair tossed back. She bent down lower to pick up her cracker, exposing more of her ample breasts.

"You're right," I said.

The dip tasted sweet and savory but also quite nutty. I washed it down with some wine.

"Hmm. Now that's different."

"Isn't it though?" she teased.

We continued to eat and chat for a few more moments before I realized something was terribly wrong.

"Excuse me," I said. "I don't feel so well."

"Maybe it's something you ate." She chuckled and now I could see her flirty smile turn sardonic. "Well, if you must know, the dip you just ate was made from horse chestnuts. Not the kind you buy in the grocery store, but the ones outside on the street that drop during the fall."

I recalled seeing them split open on the sidewalks growing up. They had a bumpy outer shell with sharp needle-like strands. But when broken open they looked just like store-bought ones cooked up for Thanksgiving. I recall my mother saying you couldn't eat them because they were poisonous.

"Actually, the biological name is Aesculus hippocastanum. And yes, they are poisonous. They cause nausea, muscle twitching and sometimes paralysis. So right now you probably wondering why I've done this, right Danny?"

I would have had answered but my mouth began to salivate and my stomach was churning. Then as if on cue, the muscles in my arms and legs began to twitch. I felt swelling in my throat. I grabbed my neck and felt unbalanced. I fell forward off the sofa onto the carpet. I could hear but couldn't speak.

"You see Danny, my father was Yoshi, the sushi chef you stole the fugu liver from. Well, he saw your video where you almost died. He felt responsible—so responsible in fact that he took his own life yesterday. He comes from a long line of proud Japanese chefs. They don't understand that often there are stupid people in the world, and that these people commit terrible acts that have nothing to do with others. There is no such thing as coincidence. Everything we do has consequences upon the universe. He felt that it was his kitchen, his fish, and his responsibility to keep others safe. He didn't wait to see the news that you actually survived your little publicity stunt. He could not live with the guilt."

At this point the twitching intensified and I wanted to throw up but couldn't. I wished there was some way to call for help, but I was powerless, and Sam was enjoying her revenge.

"So right about now, I'm sure you are wondering if I'll call 911. Not just yet. You see, I'm not really a lawyer. I have a graduate degree in psychopharmacology. I've done my research. The dose of horse chestnut I gave you won't kill you. It will just make you violently ill for a few hours. You won't die, but you may feel like you want to."

Sam folded her arms and sipped her wine slowly as I twitched and writhed on the floor. I lost all track of time. It could have been minutes or hours, but as she had promised, the symptoms gradually abated. Before I could regain my strength, however, she dragged me by my legs and dumped me outside of her door in the hall. Before she closed it she said, "Goodbye, Danny English. I suggest you find a new profession. Oh, and don't worry about the neighbors. They've seen me toss out a few drunk boyfriends before." And with that the door slammed shut.

A few months later I am sitting in an Uber cab. I'm the driver, not a passenger. Hey, I needed to do something to pay the bills. My body and head were still spinning from recent events and how quickly my life could have gone from a pinnacle into the toilet. I pick up a fare at Faneuil Hall Marketplace—a couple from New Hampshire in town to do some Christmas shopping. They are heading over to the aquarium. We make small talk and about halfway there, the husband asks me, "Hey, aren't you the guy who was writing that Deadly Foods blog a couple of months ago?"

"No," I said. "But I get that a lot. It must be my twin brother."

"Maybe. I wonder what happened to him. You never hear about him anymore. It's like he dropped off the face of the earth or something. Or maybe he died and we never heard about it."

I glanced at him in the rearview mirror and gathered my thoughts. He is staring at me, waiting for an answer.

"Yeah, I wonder about that too. Maybe he just ate too much bad food and decided to make a new career choice."

He and his wife look at each other and seem to accept my answer.

"Yeah, you're probably right," he said. "That guy was nuts and I am sure whatever happened didn't end well."

He was, of course, correct.

Dog Sense

He never thought of his dog as brilliant. Kimbo was smart, but not exceptional, not like those dogs in YouTube videos or the ones doing stupid pet tricks on late night network television. But brilliant could not describe the pet's uncanny ability to predict a fatal accident. That was magical, otherworldly.

Sarah, their next-door neighbor, "suddenly" developed a dog dander allergy, and had been its first owner. Mark was suspicious that the Golden Retriever was somehow defective. With two small children, and a third on the way, Mark and his wife, Dana, were not looking for another mouth to feed, even if it ate the same cheap food every day. However, when Sarah appeared at their door with the hyperactive puppy in tow, his two daughters exploded in excitement.

"Oh please, Dad!" Nancy shrieked. "He's so cute! We'll take care of him every day."

Not bad for a precocious eight-year-old, Mark thought. *She has a future in sales.* Her younger sibling, Monica, quiet and pudgier, nodded her head up and down, adding a modicum of credibility to her older sister's lobbying efforts.

"Well, at least he's had his shots and is housebroken, isn't he?" Dana asked Sarah.

"Yes," she said, "and he's great with kids. My nieces and nephews love him."

"What's his name?" Mark asked.

"Kimbo."

Strange name for a dog, he thought.

Mark felt an impending "Sophie's choice." Deny his children the pet and he would be forever marked in their minds as mean and heartless. Accept the offer, and he knew that he and Dana would end up walking, training, and paying vet bills for at least a decade.

It was the nonstop wagging of Kimbo's tail and incessant licking of toes and feet that sealed the deal.

"All right, all right!" Mark shouted, arms held high in the air. Glancing at Dana for support or suggestions, he saw in her eyes the unmistakable stare that said, *"It's your call buddy. This one's on you. Don't blame me if it doesn't work out."*

"We'll take him," he said reluctantly to Sarah. Turning to his children, he threw down the gauntlet, knowing it would be hard to enforce.

"One of you will walk him twice a day and make sure there is always food and water in his bowl."

Both girls nodded their heads up and down vigorously. Mark reached over to grab Kimbo's leash, but before he could grip it, the dog exploded into the front hall, rose on hind legs, and licked Nancy's chin, almost tipping her over. Both girls then raced around the den, Kimbo in hot pursuit panting, his leash lagging behind. Rivulets of dog drool dripped everywhere.

That was two years ago.

The morning of March 29 Mark arose at six and did his usual three mile run—rain, shine, snow, sleet or whatever. Every male in his family had died suddenly of heart disease before the age of sixty. He was determined not to be a statistic. He had given up smoking ten years ago, watched his diet carefully, swallowed an aspirin daily, and had exactly one glass of red wine every night with dinner.

"I don't suppose you want some pancakes and bacon that I made for the girls?" asked Dana as he returned from his run. It was a rhetorical question, of course.

"No thanks," he answered. "I'll stick with my yogurt and granola."

"Don't you get sick of eating the same thing every day?"

"I don't," he said.

"You don't get sick of eating the same thing everyday?"

No. I don't eat the same thing every day. Sometimes I eat oatmeal," he said, grinning.

He tried to leave the house by 7:30 so he could be at his

Seattle office by 9:00. He was an Amazon marketing specialist and loved his job. There was nothing better than getting paid well to sell crap to people online, creating desires for items they otherwise would never have gotten off their rumps to buy at the mall. The traffic was always unpredictable from their small Mercer Island home into the city. The morning fog began to roll in and a light drizzle ensued. Dana, on maternity leave as an intensive care unit nurse at Harborview Hospital in Seattle, would shuttle the girls to school.

"Somebody has to walk Kimbo," she shouted upstairs to the girls around seven.

"I did it yesterday," wailed Monica.

"I did it for two days in a row before that," Nancy shot back.

Soon an endless banter escalated until Mark yelled.

"Enough already! I'll do it."

As he reached for Kimbo's leash, he glared at Dana.

"This is what I told you would happen."

Dana said nothing. She continued to wash dishes and pack lunches.

Kimbo was always up for a walk, no matter what the content of his bladder or bowels. But this morning was different. As soon as he saw the leash, he cocked his head to one side and just stared. Dana glanced over her plush bathrobe-ensconced shoulder, and shrugged.

"Ok," Mark said to the dog, "What is it today?"

He waited as if the beast could actually answer. Finally, he reached over, clipped the leash to his collar, and started to move towards the door. Kimbo put on the brakes.

"What is wrong with you? You always love going for walks."

"Maybe he' s afraid of the fog," Dana opined.

"He's lived in Seattle for two years," Mark shot back, frustrated. "He's used to fog and rain."

The dog just stared, his tail down in a submissive posture—unrelenting. Mark decided to change tactics. Kneeling down, he gave him a good head pat and back rub, diving his fingers into the golden fur as an inducement. The dog maintained his catatonia and wouldn't budge.

Finally, he dropped the leash and made a move towards the door. Turning his head, he gave the pet a final warning.

"This is it—last chance. When I walk out that door you'll be alone for a few hours, and your eyeballs can float in piss for all I care."

Kimbo sat frozen, statue-like. Mark made his move to the door, and when one hand grabbed the knob, a cold nose touched the other.

"All right then. Let's roll," he said picking up the leash.

Kimbo lollygagged towards the door, in no particular hurry. They finally made it outside into the fog, which hugged the ground like a blanket. Small drops of rain floated onto their faces.

He couldn't remember a longer dog walk in his life. It must have taken at least 30 minutes by the time the animal had fully relieved himself, marking every bush, signpost, tree, and hydrant. Coming back to the yard, Mark disposed of the doggie poop bag in the trashcan along the side of the house. He swept his damp shoes on the porcupine bristle brush by the front door, re-entered, and reached for his now cold mug of coffee after washing his hands. That's when the whining started.

Kimbo barked, but Mark had never heard him whine. It was an unnatural sound that reminded him of a howler monkey, or a cat in heat.

"What is wrong with you boy?" Mark knelt down, rubbing Kimbo's face and jowls.

The dog continued to whine and now started to shiver. Mark bent down and touched every leg, belly, and back, trying to elicit a trigger point for pain. He even ran his fingers over each paw. At no point did the crying get better or worse. Dana and the girls had already left for school.

"I've got to go. If you keep this up, you're going to the vet later. Ciao."

Exiting the door, the weeping and whining only grew louder. It sounded like a refrigerator had landed on the poor thing. He glanced back for a moment, and then walked about fifty yards to his neighbor's house, leaving the front door ajar.

He knocked on the large oak door a few times and was about to walk away when it opened. Standing there in a robe was Helena, his neighbor, a tall Scandinavian woman with a latte in her hand. Her husband, Karl, was actually their vet.

"I'm sorry to bother you, but Kimbo has been acting strange this morning, and for some reason he won't stop whining and crying. I'm sure he'll stop soon, but I didn't want you to be alarmed. If he doesn't stop, I'll have Dana take him into Karl later. I have no idea what's wrong."

"Sure. It's no problem," Helena said. "Do you want to bring him over to stay with me for a while?"

"I hate to intrude and it's probably nothing ..."

Before he could finish, Helena interrupted, "It's no problem. I'll keep an eye on him."

Shuffling back through the haze, he opened the door and found Kimbo wagging his tail. The crying had stopped.

"You're unbelievable. If I didn't know better, I'd say you've been jerking my chain. You're going next door and Helena can put up with your doggie drama."

Kimbo moved to Mark's side, his tail still wagging as if nothing was wrong. He pranced ahead and was at the door well before Mark. Helena smiled and Mark looked sheepish.

"I feel stupid. He seems fine now,"

"Don't worry. I'm sure it's nothing. Now just get going."

"I can't thank you enough," Mark said, beating a hasty retreat, just in case the canine changed his mind and started yelping again.

Inside his BMW M3 sedan, he flicked on the seat warmer, lights, wipers, and sent Dana a quick text message.

<Don't know what's up with Kimbo—being PIA. Now 30 min late 4 work. He's with Helena. TTUL>

He tapped his phone's Amazon Music Library and started playing Bruno Mars on the radio. Then he spun out of the long driveway.

The cruise boat pulled away from the dock in Kirkland and headed south for its daily tour of Lake Washington. Unless the fog lifted, there would be poor views of Mt. Rainier and the Washington Huskies' football stadium. The boat was less than half full. The forecast had been iffy but the cruise operator was reluctant to cancel it as long as he had paying customers. The usual pilot, Brett Morton, had called in sick—home with the flu. The cruise operator was in a pinch. So at the last moment he called Stan Boland to pilot the boat. Stan was a private guy with a pilot license, and although he didn't sub often, he should have been able to handle it.

Had the cruise company's owner investigated, which he did not, he would have learned that Stan's license had been deactivated a month ago due to a DUI. The case was still pending but the US Coast Guard had found out about the case and issued a temporary suspension of his captain's license. When Stan got the call that morning, he didn't think to bring it up, as he was severely hung over. Gulping down three cups of coffee didn't help the heaviness above his brows, so before leaving his apartment he did two lines of coke. That did the trick and he felt alert enough to drive to the pier.

As he reached the approach to the SR 520 Bridge over the lake, Mark groaned. There was a long line of cars, and traffic was at a virtual standstill. He switched to AM radio and found out there were no accidents, but that the dense fog had slowed traffic on all the arteries into the city. Glancing at his wristwatch, he knew he was powerless to do anything. He thought about calling or emailing his office about being late but before he could pull out his phone to do this, the long line of cars began to move.

Stan steered the long boat away from the dock and relied on radar to navigate. An attendant gave safety announcements to the few tourists foolhardy enough to slog down the wharf and embark out into the cold and mist.

After thirty minutes of slow pushing through the dark water, his cell phone rang. The number was his attorney. His head clearer, he hit the boat autopilot button and took the call. That was a mistake.

The speed limit over the bridge was fifty mph. Mark was lucky if he could get to twenty. However, he was thankful that he was even moving. There was some stop and start, but mostly he was able to coast along in the left lane, barely able to see beyond one car. Punching the radio mode selector button on his steering column, he switched to a music station. That was when he heard it. At first it sounded like a thunderclap, then a bomb. Following those sounds was the unmistakable gnash of metal on metal, tires squealing, and water splashing. Instinctively, his foot squeezed the brake pedal.

Less than one minute into Stan's phone conversation, he was thrown into the windshield of the boat's helm. He immediately lost consciousness. The last sound he heard was metal hitting concrete and people screaming. His body would later be dredged from the lake, along with that of fifteen other unlucky passengers.

As his BMW came to a halt, the fog had lifted enough for Mark to see that in front of him were no bridge and no road. Two cars were perched perilously over a jagged edge that now pointed straight down into the dark abyss. People were crying and shouting. Stunned, he could only sit there, hands frozen in place on the wheel. As he removed his foot from the brake, he realized the car was tilting down towards the water. Gravity was winning. He quickly pulled the handbrake and jumped out of the sedan, running away from the gaping hole as far and as quickly as he could. He did not look back. If he had, he would have seen his M3 pitch forward and plunge out of sight.

Mark recalled helicopters, state police, coast guard, and ambulances. After refusing an interview with a local bleached blonde news reporter who shoved a microphone in his face, a policewoman grabbed his arm and gently escorted him to the back of her patrol car. He consented to a brief interview by her but had little to offer as evidence for the cause of the bridge collapse. She offered him an ambulance, but he opted for a taxi home instead. He was unable to recall anything about the ride home.

Soon the news spread over the entire Seattle area and beyond. Twitter and social media were abuzz with the accident and updates. After dropping the girls off at school, Helena was just pulling into the driveway when she heard about it on the radio. She immediately called Mark's phone. There was no answer because Mark's new iPhone was inside a very expensive German automobile at the bottom of Lake Washington. She entered the house in a panic. Looking around for Kimbo, she remembered his text message and raced next door. Before she could knock on the door, a taxi pulled into their driveway. Her shocked, wet, and quiet husband emerged from the back seat and she flung her arms around him.

That evening, Kimbo was glued to Mark. He wouldn't leave Mark's side and whined outside the door when Mark went into the bathroom. Coddling a brandy in the kitchen after the girls had gone to bed, he began to tell Dana about the dog's strange behavior that morning.

"You're saying he knew if you left too soon you would have been killed?" Dana asked.

"I'm not sure. All I know is that if I had left thirty seconds before I did, I wouldn't be sitting here now. He's never acted like that before. He purposely delayed me from going, so either this was one colossal coincidence or our dog is psychic."

Dana did not answer. They both sipped drinks. A very quiet and comfortable dog was stretched out under the table between the two of them. Mark saw two furry ears pick up and a tail wag.

Light & Dark

A Conversation

She: "What are we doing?"

He: "Going out to dinner with friends. We've already discussed it."

"No. I mean doing about us."

"There's nothing to talk about."

"That's because you won't talk about it."

He quickly held her gaze, barely making eye contact—instead choosing to focus on one of her silver hoop earrings. But she wouldn't give up.

"We can't fix this marriage unless we talk."

"We've talked and talked and nothing gets better. I can't make what we lost come back."

"No, you can't. But if we could share each other's grief, then maybe the burden would lessen. That's what couples do—you know. Besides, you haven't made love to me in months. Are you having an affair?"

He answered too quickly: "No."

Shifting on the couch, it seemed like her clothes and even the air were too heavy for her. She wished she could be lighter. It was a deep internal burden that needed easing. Her whole soul and spirit ached.

He wanted to ease her load but was incapable of moving past his own wall. He would try to soothe her.

"The doctor said it was nobody's fault, you know. It was just an unfortunate accident. With the congenital abnormality, something bad would have happened sooner or later."

"But if we had only ..."

"Stop. Please. We can't keep doing this. Nothing changes."

"The therapist says we can't heal unless we go through it."

Silence. His hands drooped to the side of the chair—exhausted. Like stone weights he brought them to his eyes and rubbed the wetness aside.

He: "What are we doing?"

She: "We're going out to dinner with friends."

Matthew's Harvest

I t was too late. When he completed medical school, any idealism he possessed was now overshadowed by $200,000 in school loans. Not anticipating the socialization of medicine by the time he ultimately became a cardiac surgeon, he could not cover all of his debts with his salary. A plumber and electrician made more per hour than he did. But that was before he met Leslie.

He was at a bar with friends and she was nursing a beer with a girlfriend. He felt a pull towards her. Excusing himself to his buddies, he sauntered over, all the while sensing a magnetic attraction. Plopping down on the stool next to her, she pretended she hadn't noticed him. He caught the bartender's eye.

"I'll have what she's having."

The bartender nodded and started to pull on the draft beer

handle. As the cold suds streamed down a tall, chilled stein, he turned towards her and said, "By the way, what are you drinking?"

Snickering and eschewing the opening gambit, she came back without hesitation, "That's one of the worst pick up lines I've ever heard."

Smiling, and not missing a beat, he shot back, "Well, how about $100 says that by the end of the night, you'll be coming home with me?"

"Even shoddier," she said. "My, you've got some big co-jones." But instead of turning away, her emerald green eyes were focused in his direction.

"You've got to be either a lawyer, a politician, or a doctor."

"Bingo," he said and extended his hand. "Dr. Matthew Samson. Pleased to meet you."

She took it firmly—more firm than he had anticipated—and said, "Leslie Perry. I'd say it's nice to meet you, but I'm not sure yet. And this is Rachel Lewis," she said as Matthew reached across her chest, careful not to touch anything, and shook her hand as well. Rachel had short-cropped black hair and little, if any, makeup.

"Les, I've got to get going—got an early court date tomorrow," Rachel said. "It was nice to meet you Dr. Samson, and good luck." Her eyes twinkled as she blew an air kiss in her girlfriend's direction and left.

"Is she a lawyer?" Matthew asked.

"No—a judge," Leslie said.

"You kidding? She looks so young."

Leslie waited a second or two, cracked a smile and said, "Got you, Doc. Yes, I'm kidding. She's a public defender."

Matthew blushed but had a quick comeback for her.

"And what do you do?"

"Oh, I work for the CIA."

Both of them laughed.

As they moved to a table, he noticed slim fingers devoid of an engagement or wedding ring, and thought *Game on*. She was rather plain, neither ugly nor beautiful. Her auburn hair was pulled back in a ponytail, and her high cheekbones accentuated her eyes and small nose. She had an ivory colored top that dove slightly, revealing a hint of cleavage. An orange and brown scarf hung lazily around her neck. A medium-length leather skirt and boots hid thick calves and a noticeable, although small, muffin-top waist.

Matthew's brown eyes fixed on hers as his curly brown hair flopped around. They made small conversation as his long arms and fingers carefully raised the beer stein for a sip.

"So," he started. "What do you really do?"

Sipping her beer she said, "Let's just say I work for a venture capitalist."

Trained to pry information out of people for his profession, he didn't stop. "That means nothing to me. You could be running illegal drugs or arms."

"And if I were, do you think I would tell someone I just met who is trying to get into my pants?"

He persisted. "No, I'm really interested."

"Why?"

"Let's just heart surgery as a profession is not what it used to be. It has evolved into a low pay, high work, and maximum bureaucratic nightmare. I'm always interested in other potential careers."

"Do you perform heart transplants?"

"Funny you should ask, but yes. Why?"

"I might have a job for you. Here's my card. Call me sometime to set up an appointment and we'll talk."

He stuffed the card in his shirt pocket without looking at it. She stood up to leave.

"Do you have to go so soon? We're just getting to know one another."

"Yes, Rachel is expecting me at home."

Matthew almost spewed out his beer. "You're a lesbian?"

"Yes dear—gotcha. By the way, you owe me a $100. She held her thumb and pinky next to her ear, emulating a telephone receiver, and mouthed the words, "Call me."

Then she was gone.

About a week later, he dropped off his dry cleaning, and Leslie's card spilled onto the floor of his car. He pulled into a parking space between the pebbles of dirt and debris and lifted it up to the light, perhaps expecting a hologram. It was vanilla-plain, like her, off-white, and had austere lettering.

Leslie Perry, Executive Vice President
"A New Life"
Personal Medical Procedures

Her phone number and address were printed below. After handing his dry cleaning bag to the woman at the drive-through window, he pulled into a parking space and dialed the number. After a few rings, she picked up.

"Leslie Perry. May I help you?"

"I don't know, but maybe I can help you. It's Matthew Samson, the surgeon you met at the bar. Remember?"

"Oh, yeah. How are you doing, Doc?"

"Fine. I'd like to speak with you more about this, uh ... opportunity."

"Sure, I'd love to have you working with us."

They arranged a time to meet the next day, late in the afternoon, when he was reasonably certain his work would be done. Then he sped off in his red Nissan 370Z.

Pulling up to the address, he was both intrigued and skeptical. The door to the office had the same name as on her card. There was dark, reflective tinting, and it was in the middle of a nondescript shopping center near an industrial part of town. He rang the bell and watched the camera watching him until she buzzed him inside. There was a single desk, phone, computer, and a faded, brown leather couch. A small sink, microwave oven, and mini-fridge in the corner completed the spartan decor. He envisioned a porn-filming studio. She pointed to a single bridge chair in front of her desk and waved for him to sit.

"Can I get you anything to drink?" she asked.

"What do you have?"

"Water, soda, ice tea, and seltzer."

"A bottle of water is fine," he said and then added, "Boy, you have a real low overhead operation here. Are you sure you can afford a heart surgeon on your payroll?"

"Yes—quite sure. What you see here is only a tiny fraction of our operation."

Sitting back in the chair and unscrewing the water cap from the plastic bottle she handed him, he said, "Now I'm really fascinated. What kind of gig is this?"

Leslie smiled and said, "Before I explain anything, I need you to sign a confidentiality agreement." Her tanned arms pushed a single page letter in his direction. It was remarkable in its brevity. It only stated that the information he would be given was private, privileged, and confidential. By signing, he agreed not to tell or share it with anyone without the company's permission, even if he chose not to accept the position. If he broke the agreement, the corporation would not hesitate to sue him.

He let out a short whistle. "Wow. You guys don't fool around. Is this necessary?"

She rocked back in her chair with hands folded in her lap and said, "I think after my presentation, you'll understand."

Matthew read the short paragraph again, muttered something under his breath that Leslie could not hear and reached for a pen in her plastic desk holder. Scribbling his name on the line and dating it, Leslie did the same as a representative of the corporation. She began with a story.

"Bob Lucas, (not his real name), was a wealthy man who seemed to have it all—family, friends, and more money than he could spend in a 100 lifetimes. How he made his fortune is irrelevant. He employed over 500 people, gave millions of dollars to charities, and was a pillar in his community. He had one flaw however—he liked to drink alcohol, too much of it. In the 1990s, he came down with cirrhosis of the liver and was also diagnosed with hepatitis C. He tried interferon therapy and all of the newest drugs but nothing helped because his liver was too damaged. By 2006, the doctors gave him only six months to live. He went to numerous transplant centers and was refused both because of his alcoholism, for which he was in and out of remission, and the enigmatic fact that even after liver transplantation, the hepatitis virus seems to recur in a majority of cases. Being used to fixing every problem he had encountered with money, he took matters into his own hands. He traveled to the Middle and Far East and assembled a team of transplant doctors who would do the service his body needed."

"But where did he get his organ?" Matthew asked.

Leslie paused for a moment, pursed her lips, leaned forward and clasped her hands.

"Life in developing countries is cheap and not as highly regarded as in the West. Let's just say families there are willing to do a lot for cash and survival."

"Are you telling me he paid to murder someone in order to harvest an organ?" Mathew asked, mouth gaping open.

"What I'm telling you is that people all over the world disappear and die for many different reasons. There is ethnic genocide, religious jihad, and unimaginable brutality among mankind. You've heard all the names: Boko Haram, ISIS, Pol Pot, Stalin, the Tutsis and Hutus. Bob Lucas was just taking advantage of a by-product of what was going to happen anyway."

"Whoa ... wait a minute," he said. "You're saying your company harvests organs from these victims before they actually die and then pays a ransom in return?"

"What I'm saying, " Leslie said sternly, "is that our company makes the best of a bad situation. The world is full of death and horror. How much is your life worth, Doctor?"

Matthew shook his head and would not answer the ethical conundrum. So Leslie did it for him.

"The answer is quite simple. It's worth whatever you or someone else is willing to pay for it."

Matthew sat stunned for a moment. He looked at his bottle of water and then her. He started to get up.

"I can't get involved in something like this. It runs completely counter to the oath I took as a doctor."

As he started towards the door, she spoke without hesitation and in an emphatic tone. "Sit down, Dr. Samson." Her tenor startled him, and he obliged. "When you do a heart transplant, do you ask or care where the donor's organ came from? You are a quarter of a million dollars in debt, like fast cars and beautiful women. How is your current position going to pay for that, may I ask?"

Torn by indecision, he stood frozen.

"We employ a very select group of professionals. Your services will be delivered in a country where, shall we say the laws are quite different then they are here in the States."

"And where would that be?"

"Have you ever heard of the Cape Verde Islands?'

"Yeah, somewhere of the west coast of Africa. I think that's where a lot of our hurricanes are born."

"Correct." She swung an iPad towards him and tapped on the screen. A professional Nat Geo-type picture of indigo waters, sandy beaches, and palm trees grabbed his eyes.

She swiped the screen with a well-polished, fire engine red fingernail and said, "This is Sal. It is the most popular island of Cape Verde, an archipelago of ten African islands located in the central Atlantic Ocean. The island of Sal, which means salt in Portuguese, is popular due to its beautiful sandy beaches. The main town is Santa Maria, where there are restaurants, bars, music, and nightlife. In short, it's paradise. Our company has built a small medical center there. Harvested organs are flown in daily, transplanted, and patients stay for several weeks recovering. Then they fly home to their respective countries for the usual post-operative care and immunosuppressive therapy. It's a cash business only. No one asks questions and everyone wins."

"Except, of course, for the poor bastards who died," Matthew said dryly.

Ignoring his comment, she persisted. "We pay our doctors one million dollars a year. They stay for one-year tours of duty with six weeks off for vacation or to visit family. The contracts renew annually only by the written consent of both parties. There is a thirty-day opt-out clause. There need be no cause or reason for both the company and the employees. If you choose to leave you must sign a non-disclosure form. Your health care will be free wherever you choose—we pay for it."

He started to nibble on the bait. "What about malpractice insurance?"

"It doesn't exist," she answered. "Our clients sign a waiver and indemnify us and all of our employees against lawsuits. Again, doctor, this is not the USA."

She could see him mulling over his options. She continued: "How well do you know the history of heart transplantation?"

"Pretty well, I guess."

"Who did the first one?"

"Dr. Christian Barnard, in South Africa."

"That's correct. Did you also know that he wasn't a heart surgeon and knew little about the organ he would soon transplant, other than what his basic medical training had afforded him?"

The doctor shook his head no.

"In fact, his hospital didn't even own the equipment to sterilize his instruments. That didn't bother him. Before his first attempt, he had wanted to transplant a black man's heart into a white man's body, but with apartheid in his country, that wouldn't pass muster. Barnard also murdered his first donor, a lady who had been hit by a truck. As the woman lay brain-dead in the intensive care unit, she was only alive due to the beating of her heart. He gave her a lethal shot of potassium that stopped her heart so he could harvest it. So you see, the whole field of transplantation was birthed out of a less than ethical environment."

Matthew thought for a moment. He was an only child, had just lost his parents in a terrible auto accident, and had no current girl friend or fiancée, although he had methodically worked his way through a whole cadre of more than willing surgical nurses, assistants, and medical students. Hell, he didn't even have a dog or cat. The ethics still nagged at him but the financial jackpot was hard to ignore.

"When would I start?"

"How much notice does your current employer need?" she asked smiling.

He delicately placed the last stitch that joined the donor's aorta to the recipient's heart. Like magic, the new heart slowly began to beat as warm blood coursed through its valves and chambers. Watching with satisfaction, he wired closed the breastbone, and finally the skin of the overweight German. Walking away from the table, he snapped off his gloves in a single motion, then his gown and mask, and pushed the aluminum operating room door outwards towards the dictation room. The medical center had an electronic medical record system, which was far easier to learn and use than any in the States. He completed his operative note via voice recognition software in less than ten minutes. Rising out of the comfortable leather chair, he strode into the doctor and nurse's lounge and pushed the button on the coffee machine. The choices were overwhelming—Jamaica Blue Mountain, Costa Rica, Sumatra, and Kona, Hawaii. There was espresso, cappuccino, and six kinds of latte. The electronic barista served up a perfect eight-ounce cup of this week's special—Ethiopian Yirgacheffee. The rich fumes sent out aromas of chocolate and nuts. Above the machine was a colorful "Coffee Taster's Wheel of Flavors," listing more than 200 ways to describe the flavor of an original bean. It was far more complicated than wine tasting.

Moving over to the large plate glass window that overlooked the sapphire blue water and pink sand beaches, he sighed at his milestone. He had just completed his 100th heart transplant in less than nine months of working in Sal. That was more than double the number he had done during his whole career and training back home.

The sound of another helicopter arriving was unmistakable. The whirring of the rotors always made him excited. Sand kicked up over the beach. He was still impressed by the unbelievable technology. The donor organs were flown in from Dakar, Senegal in special ice chests. The short trip of 400 miles took only a couple of hours with the new speedier choppers.

How the organs, or bodies, made it to Dakar for harvesting, he did not want to know. Some small part of his brain still questioned the ethics of his work. However, the fact that he had already paid off his school loans and was debt free removed a tremendous burden from his shoulders. He had a beach condo, a Ferrari convertible, and a Harley Davidson motorcycle. The sun shone 350 days a year and the temperatures were always mild, 70 to 80 degrees on most days. Matthew's only complaint was the limitations of his bachelorhood. He steered cleared of the native women, and many of the medical staff was married. Margot had become his "go-to" gal.

A tall, bronze-skinned OR nurse from Portugal, she was fluent in three languages: Spanish, English, and Portuguese. She was five years older than he, divorced but with no children. She ran eight miles on the beach daily and was a fantastic physical specimen for someone pushing 40. And in bed, they never tired of sex. Although she had a small apartment inland, they had been cohabitating for weeks. In short, Matthew was truly living his dream.

"Another beautiful day in paradise," she said, touching his shoulder. He turned from the window and gave her a quick hug and cheek kiss. Internal dating was not forbidden by the company but was frowned upon. There was a pragmatic acknowledgment that it could hardly be prevented.

"What do you want to do for dinner?" he asked.

"We've eaten out a lot—how about I cook you some fresh

fish baked in banana leaves?"

She was an expert in the kitchen and he said yes without hesitation. "I'll see you back at my place after work. We'll have some drinks, dinner, and watch the sun set," he said. "Okay?"

"It sounds perfect to me."

She pivoted in her lime-green scrubs and clacked away in wooden clogs that raised her two inches taller than normal. Her long brown hair bounced softly on her shoulders.

As they sat sipping cocktails on his porch, Margot encircled his neck with her strong arms. They were both relaxed and looked out over the still waters. Her bikini top revealed ample tan cleavage. Her bottom was covered with a floral, cotton skirt, split on one side, revealing a long muscular leg. The azure seas slowly engulfed the setting golden sun.

"How about a ride before dinner?" he asked.

"Sure."

As they mounted his Harley, Margot placed the heavy black helmet on her head. Before he turned the key, she whispered in his ear, "Matthew, your helmet."

"Not tonight. It's so warm, and that thing's too confining. I have to buy a lighter one. Besides, it's only a short ride, and there's no traffic." She learned not to argue but was uncomfortable with his answer. Ever since they had met, he had always worn his helmet. There was no law in Sal about helmets, however.

They zipped around the curvy mountain road, and every hairpin turn gave successive views of the beach, as orange, red, and yellow shadows melded into the ocean horizon. As light faded fast, his automatic headlight turned on. Monkeys swung from a banana tree along the side of the road and Matthew pointed and turned to show her.

It was an instant—surely less than a second. He did not see the old, native man tugging a stubborn donkey and cart across the road. By the time he saw him, it was too late. He slammed on his brakes, broke to the right, and narrowly missed them. However, the large boulder on the shoulder was unavoidable. He spun the bike to the right again but the front wheel struck the immovable giant, ejecting both driver and passenger into the air and down the ravine.

Despite her helmet, Margot was killed instantly as a splintered tree trunk entered her spleen, lung, and heart. For a moment, Matthew's only world was pain—and it was everywhere. He was sure both his legs were broken, ribs cracked, and his head throbbed. He tasted the salty and copper flavor of his own blood dripping down his face into his mouth. He was choking on it and could not clear his airway. Before he passed out, he saw nothing but white—so white it was blinding—and seemed to stretch on forever. He lost tract of time; seconds, minutes, or even hours of intense pain dragged on. He was unaware of the bystanders, the paramedics, and finally the helicopter when it lifted him out of the canyon.

"I have a pulse, but no blood pressure!" screamed a paramedic.

"He needs IV fluids and blood stat!" yelled another one.

"Christ, I can't even start an IV for that—he needs a central line."

Back and forth the dialogue went until there was no longer a pulse or heartbeat. By this time, Matthew's body was in the chopper and the crew began CPR. A tube was shoved down his throat, and a copious amount of blood was suctioned out through it. Oxygen was pumped into his lungs as one of the medics pushed methodically on his chest. Finally a decent heartbeat was restored. It took only a few minutes to get to the medical center, and as the bird landed on the roof, doctors and nurses swarmed his stretcher. One of the docs was able to establish a central vein conduit under his collarbone and fluids were poured in. Suddenly Matthew's heart began to beat. Battered, broken, and bruised, he was rushed into the ICU.

With emergency surgery, a burst blood vessel outside his brain was repaired. Next, under his skull where gobs of clots had been trapped, they suctioned the delicate tissue. His belly was also sliced open and a bleeding spleen removed. For the moment, at least, he was stabilized. His broken leg bones would have to wait for another day. But that day would never come.

Matthew never woke up. Hours stretched into days, and then days into weeks. A distant cousin back in the States, who hadn't seen him in over ten years but was his only recorded next of kin, was contacted. Matthew's EEG, or brainwave test, showed no meaningful activity. Ironically, his heart continued to beat by itself—regular and strong. His body would recover, but his brain would not. It was dead. Only a beating heart and life support maintained a charade of real life.

And so Matthew Samson, heart doctor, American ex-patriot, and cardiac surgical mercenary, would become an organ donor. Five weeks after the accident, another surgeon harvested his heart. It was successfully inserted into the chest cavity of an African dictator, who neither asked nor cared where it had come from.

Light & Dark

In the Ocean

Every mouthful of air tasted like salt. My head, torso, and limbs went numb as I bobbed up and down. Clinging to an ice cooler, all I could think about was the self-inflating life vest I had never worn. Ten feet. That's all that separated me on board from wearing the safety harness—that and a heavy dose of unbridled hubris. I watched as my boat began to sink slowly into the Gulf of Mexico. It was as if a giant fish was slurping it up with a wet tongue.

"If you're going out alone to fish, make sure to put on your life vest," she would always say. "I don't want to be a widow."

I nodded, but never intended to follow her command.

It was likely due to "testosterone poisoning," another one of her favorite phrases. *No*, I thought. *It's not that. It's denial. It will happen to someone else but never to me.*

Seconds blended into minutes and then hours. There had not been enough time to send a radio distress call. Being spring, the water was seventy-two degrees—enough to induce hypothermia. Hugging my Yeti cooler, I began to hallucinate. First I saw a rescue boat and then a helicopter. Day slipped into dusk and I could no longer feel my fingertips. My first fear had not been of drowning, but rather eaten by a shark. But when I felt the bump on my leg, I assumed I was imagining this too. Then it bumped again, but stronger. I braced for the pain of a bite and waited. Nothing.

I was only an average swimmer and was ten miles from shore. There was no way I could swim half that distance, even with an adrenaline surge. I would kick every few minutes just to feel my legs. I had to hug the cooler with more of my arms since my fingers were now numb.

The seas built and I became dizzy and nauseous.

A hum grew louder and louder. Was it above or below me? I couldn't tell.

Then a bright light emerged from the sky. This is it, I thought—death.

A voice called my name.

"Grab the cradle! It's above you! Look up!"

Hook

Owen "Fishhook" Jones sat on his favorite seawall overlooking the bay. The day was cool, a bit breezy, and overcast—typical for March on the west coast of Florida. Although his nickname was Fishhook, most of his friends and acquaintances simply called him Hook. Few, if any, people called him Owen, and almost no one knew his past or where he lived. They did, however, know that he fished from the same seawall every day. It was hard to tell his exact age, since his dark skin never seemed to change color even though his hair was starting to gray. He had few wrinkles, which he attributed not to sunscreen, for he used none, but the old adage, "Black don't crack."

A rusty-colored feral cat hung around as he discarded bits of shrimp, whitebait, or fish scraps. He just called it "Cat." A statuesque egret stood next to him almost daily as well, looking for a free meal. Her sharp, orange beak accented her slender neck. Hook named her "Roberta," although he had never known a "Roberta" and didn't even know if she was female.

His battered Coleman cooler, cast nets, tackle box, and fishing pole were constant companions. His old beach bike had been retrofitted with PVC piping for his pole and a clapboard trailer for his other gear. He kept a plastic yellow poncho that he had found at the Goodwill store for five dollars in case it rained, which was sudden and often in Florida.

Locals, school kids, and tourists would try to engage Hook in conversation. It wasn't that he was unfriendly. He just didn't feel much like talking most of the time. He could sense and smell fish almost mystically. He kept two cast nets by his side: one was for whitebait, otherwise known in Florida as scaled sardines or "shiners." They were scarce in the winter and plentiful in the summer. The other was larger and he used that for gathering up mullet. These he mostly sold at the local fish stores and kept some for smoking.

Mullet are bony vegetarian fish that travel in packs, often leaping out of the water for reasons unknown but often speculated upon. They were easy to catch with the proper net, but not so easy to haul up over a seawall.

As he gazed out on the water, he saw some dolphins feeding which was both a good and bad sign. It was good because it meant fish were in the area, and bad because the fish sensed the hunters' presence and usually wouldn't feed until they were gone. The mullet didn't care. They were too stupid to swim away.

"What are you fishing for?" a voice asked.

Hook saw a teenage boy on a skateboard staring at him intently.

"Anything that will bite."

"You know snook are out of season." The boy said this with authority.

Hook cracked a sideways smile and said, "You don't say."

"Do you mind if I watch?"

"Suit yourself," said Hook.

The fisherman stabbed another piece of PVC into the soft grass and used it for a rod holder. He then reached for his plastic, yellow shrimp bucket that was dangling by a rope in the water and picked out a medium-sized brown critter. He carefully placed the point of a circle hook under the horn of the shrimp and then cast it far off towards the murky, dark water. It landed with a gentle *plop*. Next, he placed the rod into the PVC holder. He reached into his cooler and withdrew a bottle of orange Gatorade and took a sip. In another bag was a snap-open can of Vienna sausages, many a fisherman's lunch staple. He chewed the rubbery little fingers of processed meat and watched the water.

After about twenty minutes, the boy said, "This is boring."

Hook didn't acknowledge him or answer, but the lad was not giving up.

"Do you use circle hooks?"

"Sometimes," he said tersely.

"Why?"

Seeing that there would be no way out of conversing he swiveled around on his small portable stool and eyed the boy directly. He looked to be around fourteen. He was tall and lanky with unkempt sandy-colored hair and jeans that hung precariously near the bottom of his slim hips.

"Well, I used to always use plain J-hooks, but a few years back I decided to try the circle hooks. The fish are more likely to be lip-hooked and not swallow them, and therefore easier to release unharmed. Also, since they let the fish hook themselves, it frees me up to do other things."

"Like eating?"

Hook nodded.

The inquisition didn't end there.

"How long you been fishin'?"

"I don't remember, but I'd say at least forty years."

"Whew," whistled the teen. "That's a lot years. You always lived here?"

"Yep, born and raised."

Suddenly, the rod bent as line began to fly off the reel. Hook dropped his sausage on the grass as Cat hurried over and gobbled it up. He grabbed the rod and started to reel.

"The thing about circle hooks is you don't set the hook. You just reel."

As he continued to reel he could feel the weight of the fish. Hook turned to the boy and said, "You want to reel her in?"

A broad smile came over his face and he nodded and hopped off his skateboard. Hook handed him the pole and said, "Now don't reel too fast, just keep tension at all times and the rod tip bent a bit."

He could see the excitement on the boy's face as he firmly gripped the old pole and reeled in as instructed. When the fish finally came close to the seawall, Hook smiled.

"A redfish. Nice job." Hook leaned over with a landing net and scooped it.

The boy beamed broadly.

Hook threw the fish on some ice in the cooler and went back to fishing. The boy watched him a while longer, but became bored again and left. Near sunset Hook began to pack up his gear. His knees cracked and popped as he rose from the ground. Before leaving his spot he had one last task. Removing an old fillet knife from his pack, he laid the fish on top of the cooler and skillfully removed each fillet from both sides. Turning the fillets over he trapped a corner of the skin under his finger and used the knife to separate the skin from the meat. He hacked off the meat with rib bones still attached and tossed it to the still waiting Roberta, who wolfed it down with one quick swallow. He could see the fish carcass distend the skinny bird's neck as it passed from beak to stomach. *If only people could be as patient as animals*, he thought.

Hook hadn't always been a full-time fisherman. He had worked hard most of his life at odd jobs—driving a cab, construction, cook, gardener, handyman, and collecting trash for the city. His worst job ever was laying roof tiles. In the summertime he could lose one to two gallons of fluid daily. He lasted only a few weeks on that job. He liked to work to keep his mind off of his childhood. That's where the real demons lived.

Raised by a single mother, his alcoholic father would return home on occasion just long enough to abuse the kids and his mom. Hook hated him. They called him Pa but Hook preferred the word "Poor" because he didn't have a job and would never bring home any food or money, although somehow he found enough cash to buy booze and smokes. Hook determined if he ever had kids he would work and support them.

As life often happens, things did not turn out that way. His wife left him for another man after only six months of marriage. He never recovered from the shame and embarrassment. He had subsequent girlfriends from time to time, but his inability to talk and communicate his feelings always left them wanting more. He finally just gave up. He knew it was wrong but when he worked and had some money, he would utilize the services of a hooker. Despite the known risks, he felt it safer than the eventual heartbreak of a normal relationship.

The next day was sunny and warmer. The clouds had cleared and an east wind gently lapped the bay and the trees. It was around sunrise—always the best time to fish in Hook's opinion. He sipped his cardboard coffee cup from the local convenience store—he liked it without sugar or cream—and munched on a donut. He caught a couple of small speckled sea trout but had to throw them back because they were undersized.

About an hour after dawn, he heard a familiar hum. A group of tourists with helmets approached on Segways. They stopped for a bit and watched him and then continued on their tour of downtown St. Pete with its new high-rise $1 million+ condos and a new crop of bars and restaurants. Sailboats scooted over the horizon on the large bay that separated Tampa from his home city. Formerly known as "the city of green benches" and "land of the newly wed and nearly dead," St. Pete had become more popular with rich baby boomers and their children and was no longer the butt of every growing old and retiring joke. Next, the bicyclists, rollerbladers, and runners streamed by in rapid succession. Everyone seemed to be in such a hurry to exercise.

Around mid-morning he noted a rippling in the water. A hairy, gray snout surfaced for air, and he noted two manatees, a mom and her pup. They were grazing on sea grass. Just behind them a school of mullet jumped as they came closer to the seawall. He dropped his pole and grabbed his large net. He readied it for a cast with a piece of rope in his mouth separating two lead weights. He watched and waited. Poised like a ballerina, he drew the carefully folded net behind him and then tossed it in front like a Frisbee. The net opened wide and flat and trapped dozens of the fish before the lead could hit the shallow bottom. He tightened the rope and pulled. The net by itself must have weighed 16 pounds and now loaded with fish, probably over 50. He lay down on the seawall and pressed his chest into the rough, warming concrete. He dragged the squirming mass to the wall and with one giant heave splayed them out on the grass. He scooped them up by the handful and tossed them into the ice chest. He was barely able to close it with a large bungee cord. There were too many, so he heaved some back into the water as a superstitious offering to the "fish gods." Gathering his equipment, he mounted his bike and rode to the fish store to sell his catch. The owner looked at his full cooler and without even weighing it, gave him five $20 bills.

Hook broke for lunch at a local hamburger joint and then returned to his spot to fish some more. As he was setting up, he noticed a commotion out of the corner of his eye. A burly man was yelling at a woman.

"Hey bitch, I told you never to see that guy again!"

"I don't know what you're talking about!" she said, trembling.

Although quite large, the man did not appear to be in very good shape. His scruffy beard and unkempt hair poked out of his New York Yankees ball cap. A large belt and loose pants could barely contain his sizeable beer belly. The woman was tiny—probably no more than five feet tall. She was disheveled and may have even been homeless. The big guy got into her face.

"I saw you talking to him last night," he yelled.

She began to cower.

"I was just getting the rest of my stuff out of his apartment for Chrissake," she pleaded.

As the space between them closed, Hook dropped his pole

and approached the arguing couple. Although he was almost six feet tall and in good physical shape, Hook was far from muscular.

"Do we have a problem here?" Hook asked from a few feet away.

The man scowled at him. "Mind your own business, pops."

Hook kept coming. "Is he bothering you, ma'am?" He judged her to be in her late twenties. Her dirty blonde hair showed dark roots. She had no makeup on, and her slender body revealed a pierced navel, cutoff jeans shorts, flip-flops, and a tattered v-neck sweater. She was afraid to speak.

"I told you to stay out of this, old man!"

As the gap closed, Hook could sense the big guy losing control. Having been in more than one fight, he knew all the signs. The man's nostrils flared and his breathing quickened. Hook didn't wait for him to strike. Instead, he reached behind and quickly withdrew a large filleting knife. One look at that and the attacker's eyes widened and his advance halted. Waving a finger at the woman, he stormed off, yelling, "You haven't seen the last of me yet!"

The woman was visibly shaken and trembling. She turned with wet eyes toward Hook and simply said, "Thank you."

"Do you need me to call the police for you?" After he said it he realized how silly the offer was since he didn't even own a mobile phone.

"No thanks. I will be all right."

She was sniffling and Hook handed her one of his clean rags.

Before saying goodbye, he offered some advice.

"Be careful who you hang with, ma'am. Guys like that are bullies. He probably won't leave you alone. Do you have some place to go that's safe?"

She simply nodded and walked away.

Growing up with an abusive father, Hook had learned to protect himself at a young age. He couldn't always fight hard but he knew when to run, and he could run fast. In fact, in high school his track coach had nicknamed him "Lightning." The name stuck for a while but Hook felt like a "step-and-fetch-it" whenever someone called him that.

He had served in the army for a few years towards the end of 'Nam. He had spent some time in jail accused of a robbery he did not commit. His mistake was being poor, hanging with the wrong guys, and having to use a public defender that made a plea deal.

As he spread out his gear the morning after the domestic dispute, the sun rose high in the sky and the warm, humid air surrounded him. Bait started to pop in the water, a sure sign of improving spring fishing. He donned his baseball cap and a yellow rubber-fishing bib and reached for his cast net. He had it slung over his shoulder, ready to toss when out of the corner of his eye when he saw a young Afro-American boy watching him. He could not have been more than ten or eleven years old. He had a dirty and stained "wife-beater" undershirt and faded beige shorts. His thin, stork-like legs ended with dime-store flip-flops. It was usually easy for him to ignore spectators, but in this case, he could not seem to get his attention from the boy although the child had said nothing.

Finally, he put down his cast net and approached the waif. "You by yourself?"

"Yes, sir."

"What's your name, boy?"

"Calvin, or Cal sir."

"Nice manners but I am not your sir. My name's Hook." He extended his callused hand to shake the boy's. The boy almost had an allergic reaction and then cautiously shook Hook's hand with a quick and guarded grip.

"Where are your people?" Hook asked.

The boy just shrugged his shoulders up to the sky and said nothing.

"Cat got your tongue?"

Again, a shrug resulted with the boy's head drooped down.

"You know anything about fishin'?"

"Nope."

"Why aren't you in school?"

Again, there was no answer as the young, dark eyes stared past Hook, very much afraid of eye contact.

"You can sit over here close to me. I won't hurt you," Hook said.

The boy nodded his head and shuffled over to a worn and splintery park bench. He watched Hook intently as the old man threw the net and hauled in a bunch of shiny whitebaits. He dumped them into a large plastic bucket with a battery-powered aerator to keep them alive longer.

"Come over here, Cal. These are shiners, or scaled sardines. Put your hand in and feel them. They won't bite and they don't have any sharp fins or gills like other fish."

The boy hesitated and watched as the man slipped his hand in the bucket and gave a gentle swirl. Convinced it was safe, he dunked his right arm into the cool water and stirred it around a bit before jerking it out.

"What's the matter?" Hook asked.

"Nothin'," the boy said as he smiled. "They feel slippery."

"Do you know why that is?"

"Nope."

"Because they're fish," Hook said, laughing to himself, hoping to crack the tough emotional curtain surrounding the boy.

"Right. Can I touch 'em again?"

"Sure," said Hook.

"Will I hurt them?"

"You might but they are going to die quickly anyway in a bigger fish's belly or in this here bucket, so go ahead. It don't matter because there are more fish in the sea," joked Hook, again laughing at himself.

The boy obviously didn't get the clichéd reference but smiled anyway. As Hook bait a hook and tossed it into the water, the boy kneeled down and continued to run his hands through the bait.

It did not take long before a pull on the rod signaled a fish swallowing fresh bait and the hook attached to it. The boy stared as the old man gently coaxed the trapped fish towards him. He asked the boy if he wanted to reel it in, but the scruffy youth just shook his head rapidly from side to side as if Hook had asked him to handle a shark. Seeing the fear in the boy's eyes, Hook brought the almost two-foot-long spotted weakfish to the seawall, reached his lanky arm and worn black net down, and scooped it up in one motion without losing his balance.

As the silver fish with black spots flopped on the grass inside the net, the boy ran behind a palm tree and hid, as if the thing might rear up and attack him. The old man laughed and gently removed the hook. As he smiled towards the tree, he said, "Come over and take a look. She won't bite you."

Cautiously, the boy walked towards his new friend but kept arm's length from the fish. He watched intently as the man reached out for his hand. After shaking his head a few times, he finally extended his trembling right hand as Hook took it and let it lie on the fish's side. The boy withdrew it quickly as if he had touched a hot stove. Hook smiled again and said, "It's okay. You'll learn they won't hurt you."

By this time the child's pupils were huge and a faint smile came over his dirty face. After placing the fish in the cooler, he turned to the boy.

"You hungry?"

He nodded yes.

Hook dug into his lunch cooler and found some smoked fish spread, old cheese, and a peanut butter and jelly sandwich. He offered them to the boy who turned up his nose at the first two and pointed to the PB&J. As they sat on the soft grass and listened to crows and wild parrots squawk above, Hook started to speak.

"You don't say much."

The boy shrugged as he gobbled down his sandwich.

"You seem a lot like me as a kid. You only talk when you have somethin' to say, right?"

Again the boy nodded yes.

"Okay. Tell you what. You come back tomorrow and maybe we'll talk and fish some more, okay?"

The boy nodded yes again but wouldn't walk away. He just sat on the sand and rough St. Augustine grass with its sharp blades and stared out at the water. After a few hours, he fell asleep. Hook arranged his windbreaker on two poles over the little guy so he wouldn't get too hot in the sun. As he was gathering all his gear to head home, the boy woke.

"You need a ride somewhere?" Hook asked.

The boy seemed to be thinking and then stammered, "I got no place to go."

"Okay, now this is serious. No more foolin' around. Where do you live?'

After a few minutes, Cal told him how he had lost his dad

to gang violence—a drive-by shooting. His mother was a crack addict and he had been turned over to the care of the State. He had not yet been placed in a foster home, so he was at some youth facility. Hook knew it well, for he had spent some time in the same place as a child.

"So you're living at Bell Place, right?"

The boy nodded.

"Are they treating you okay?

"I guess," the boy said in a most unconvincing tone.

"Well, we've got to get you back there. It's almost dark. Those folks will be worried about you."

"No they won't," Cal said. Unfortunately, Hook knew he was right.

Cal sat on top of the fish cooler as Hook pedaled slowly through the streets. Cal tightly grabbed the taut bungee cord like it was reins on a bucking bull. The sun was beginning to set and over the water were stacked layers of orange, yellow, blue and red color bands and wispy clouds. The sea breeze was picking up. The youth home was only a few miles away and they arrived at dusk.

Hook rang the bell several times before anyone answered. He looked around at the old brick walkway and porch, now tinted green with algae and black mildew. The cracked white plaster on the side of home was now gray and peeling. The rusty door creaked open.

"Yes?" An older Afro-American woman with gray hair and a faded black apron cracked the door a bit and stuck her head

part of the way out. She was probably over 250 pounds and tee-
tered on weak and arthritic knees. Her beige hose and sneakers
looked like they had been worn every day for months.

"Are you missing someone?" Hook asked as he gently
pushed the door back and showed her Cal, who was cowering
by his side.

"Oh Cal, you ran away again?"

That's it?, Hook thought.

With his head bent down, the boy walked inside.

"You're too late for dinner but I'll see what I can get rustled
up," the rotund woman said.

"Make sure he gets a bath, too," said Hook.

Indignant, the woman rifled back, "Who are you, a relative?"

"No," said Hook. "I'm just someone who cares, which is
more than he probably has at this place."

The door slammed in his face, and he walked away.

He awoke to a *rat-a-tat-tat*. The rain fell like bullets on his
tin roof. Even acorns falling off oak trees sounded like bombs
through the thin sheet metal. But it had kept Hook dry for many
years and he wasn't about to change it—not that he could, even
if he wanted to since he had little money. He looked down at
his hard toenails and thought that soon he would need a metal
file to take care of them if they got any thicker. Thunder had
awakened him early and he looked out of his old, slatted jal-
ousie windows. The only thing that ever kept him from fishing

was lightning. He had a healthy respect for nature and that was one risk he wasn't willing to take. The storm passed quickly as the wind picked up from the north, signaling one last gasp of Florida's winter from a weakened cold front.

He put up a pot of coffee in an old tin percolator and squeezed some oranges for juice. Then he made grits, fried up some bacon and followed that with two fried eggs over easy—the same breakfast he'd had for thirty years. As he ate, he watched the palm trees bending with the wind. He did not have a television or a computer, but he did have an old plug-in radio. If a stranger had entered his small one-bedroom house at that moment and looked around, they would likely think it odd that this crusty old man listened to public radio.

As the news finished on NPR's "Morning Edition," he cleaned up his dishes and put on an old denim shirt. The same faded jeans he had worn for the past week beckoned him from the floor. Socks and underwear was the only thing he changed daily. He brushed his teeth in front of an old mirror that had long ago lost most of its silver. He stared at his gnarly gray beard and thought about Calvin. The boy's entrance into his life was bothersome. It wasn't that the boy would be trouble, but more that he reminded Hook too much of himself. And that was something he took little comfort in.

The humidity was dropping as he biked to his fishing spot. Soon the spring and summer would enter with the oppressive damp atmosphere that his body had adapted to long ago. As he parked his bike under the same live oak tree, he noticed a figure on the seawall. He sighed and approached slowly. Calvin looked up.

"Why did you talk to my people at the foster home yesterday?"

"Because I was worried about you," Hook responded.

"Nobody else does. I'll be okay."

"I'm not so sure about that."

The two then sat in silence and fished. Hook showed him how to bait the hook and cast the line out far into the water. He showed him how to patiently wait for the fish to take the bait before setting the hook.

"Remember," Hook said. "Crank—don't yank."

The boy nodded.

They caught some small speckled trout that they threw back. Calvin was getting used to the jumpy shrimp and the slimy fish. The boy was a quick learner and soon became less squeamish.

As the sun peaked through the clouds, the wind picked up more and soon the walkers, runners, and bikers were out in growing numbers. Hook removed a wad of Redman chewing tobacco from his pocket and slid it under his tongue. It was his only vice and he was certain that ultimately it would cause his death.

"What's that stuff you eatin'?" Cal asked.

"It's chewing tobacco and it's a nasty habit. Don't even think about starting it and don't ask me anymore about it." Hook was ashamed of his inability to curb his addiction. He had quit drugs and alcohol a long time ago but felt embarrassed that he couldn't give up his "chew."

The boy looked away as if just watching his new friend's addiction might be contagious. Hook grabbed a used Ziploc plastic bag and spat a hunk of dark gunk inside. After a few seconds, Cal asked him, "Why don't you just stop?"

"I thought I told you not to ask me about it," Hook said, annoyed.

The boy shrugged and turned his attention back to his fishing pole.

"Is there anything you really like to eat?" Hook asked.

"Fruit Loops," said the boy.

"So why don't you give up eating them?"

"Because I like 'em." And then as if he had read the old man's mind, he added, "Besides, they ain't goin' to kill me."

Hook sat in silence. He spit out the rest of his wad. Calvin offered him a stick of old mint gum. Hook smiled and took it with grace. As they both smiled the boy said, "Fishin' is slow today."

"I believe you're right," said Hook. "Some days are like that, you know?"

"I know," said the boy. "But tomorrow will probably be better."

Hook said nothing. He just ran his roughened fingers through the boy's hair and smiled.

Light & Dark

The Chair

Although I have no say in the matter, I will soon be reborn. Again, it is not of my choosing but I have heard the talk. I am not sure of the exact date or what it will feel like, but I sense that it will be soon. This event got me to remember all of what I have been through in my lifetime. Some have been pleasant, some sad, and some downright horrible.

I remember every time someone sat on me and what he or she felt like and what was said. As time has worn on, my wooden bones are a bit weaker with a few splinters and many scratches. My fabric has worn down and the edges have been smoothed over like sandpaper.

There is an unfortunate cigarette burn on my left arm from that dreadful teenager Sam who dated our beautiful Melissa. It happened, of course, when the parents weren't home. She got grounded for a week after that one but the burnt wood indentation still smarts.

Then there was grandpa who would sit and watch football for hours and holler, "Hey Ref, get some glasses! Can't you see that was pass interference?" His wife, Sadie must have weighed four hundred pounds. My, I thought my legs would break.

Or Aunt Jamie, who would drink a pint of vodka in a single sitting and pass out. Thank goodness she never had a body fluid accident on me. And while we are on that subject there was that awful episode when the kids were gone. Mom and Dad decided to enjoy a moment of conjugal bliss spontaneously on my wide and supple seat. They must have scrubbed me for hours to get that awful sticky substance off before Melissa and Jamie came home.

I don't hate animals but that awful Persian cat, (what was her name?), shed all over me. Although I must admit that the feel of the vacuum cleaner massaging me was just sublime. I didn't mind Ralph, the poodle, because he didn't shed. But I couldn't stand it went he bent over to lick his balls.

So many people and animals have used me. I have been a receptacle for laptops, shoes, toys, chewed up bones, and even a fishing tackle box. I have been subjected to dirt, skin, snow, mud, and water. The worst (other than the sexual escapade of course) was when father spilt his coffee all over me. They had to call in a professional for that one.

But my end of time is coming soon. It won't be Goodwill or

the Salvation Army. I haven't heard mention of eBay or Craigslist either. But there are whispers of the one thing we all dread: reupholster.

Light & Dark

The Art of Jumping

I am sweating and the torrents of water will not stop. Although the temperature is over ninety degrees, I am also shivering. As I look at the sandpit, I gauge the distance to be thirty feet or more. My personal best is twenty-five feet. I shake my head to release the rivulets off my face and out of my eyes. With my head down, I glance at the judge who gives me a nod, signaling it's okay to start. With my spikes dug into the grass, I pitch forward, like a horse out of the starting gate. At this point, there is no thinking, for my body is on autopilot. I approach the granular pit rimmed in wood and launch into the air. It seems like I'm airborne forever, but I know it is only seconds. The jump feels good and for the briefest moment, I am neither hot nor cold. I land awkwardly, my right ankle screaming at me. Pitching to my side, I grab my leg and roll forward.

The adrenaline coursing through my veins helps abate the pain.

"Twenty-five feet, six inches!" yells the judge. Good, but maybe not good enough to get me past the Olympic-qualifying trials. I limp out of the pit towards the side of the field. My coach, Hector "Hex" Gonzales, hands me a towel and bottle of water.

"Better."

He's tall and lanky with slicked, jet-black hair and brown skin. He gives no indication of success or failure. He doesn't ask about the pain. I don't complain because I know he doesn't care. It's not that he doesn't care about me as a person, it's just that he has many students. Pain and injuries are just troublesome obstacles on the road to victory.

"Can you jump again today?"

"No," I say.

As I rise out of my bed, I feel the familiar pain and numbness on my left side. My arm feels worse than my leg, but neither is good. My physical therapist, Katie Jordan, will be over shortly.

"Can I get you a cup of coffee?" asks my wife, Marie.

"Sure. But make sure it's hot and not warm," I snap. I am angry that I have again been short with her.

I am anticipating another day of hellish PT and am in a grumpy mood. It is a month since my stroke and I am impatient to be feeling better. My dog, Dutch, is at my feet, resting with his head on my leg. I wonder how dogs know what part of your body is injured or hurt. The doorbell rings and Marie yells, "I'll get it!" I glance towards the streaming sunlight, expecting to see perky Katie. Instead, there is a stocky, middle-aged man with stringy red hair.

"May I help you?" My wife asks.

He extends a hand. "I'm Michael Dunbar, a physical therapist. Katie is ill today. May I come in?"

He walks in cautiously, scanning our modest living room, looking around as if something might attack him. Then he looks at me and smiles.

"You must be Jason?"

We shake hands and again I'm thankful for being right-handed so I don't have to extend a limp limb. Inside, I'm seething. The only word I can think of is *gimp*.

"Jason Langley," he says. "You won the triple jumping crown at the 2002 Salt Lake City Olympics, right?"

I nod my head, almost in shame. Then I try some levity.

"That was a long time ago. Now I'd be lucky to jump over a cardboard box from Amazon."

"And that is precisely what our goal will be this week."

"I was joking."

"Perhaps," he says. "But I'm not."

I like him already.

The Triple Jump crown is defined by winning the long jump, the high jump, and the triple jump. Few have done it. I did it in 2002. Most people with a cursory knowledge of such things know what the long and high jumps are since they are self-explanatory. But the triple jump is more obscure. Much like the long jump, the triple jump begins along a narrow track. The athlete must sprint toward three designated zones, marked by lines, before jumping for distance. The jumper must touch down with one foot in each zone before launching for distance into the sandbox. The jumping sequence is commonly referred to as the hop, step, and jump phase.

My success was brief and I did get some short-lived commercial endorsements, like being on a cereal box. But fame, like most other things in life, is fleeting. Three years later, at the qualifying trials for the 2006 games in Turin, Italy, I tore my Achilles tendon. In less time than it takes to apply brakes on a car, my Olympic career came to a screeching halt. Fortunately, I still had a day job.

The funny thing about strokes is that one minute you are well, and the next minute you are not. I suspect that most stroke and heart attack victims feel the same. They can remember the precise second before it happened—what they were dong and where they were. And while we're on the subject, let's talk about victimhood. My therapist (psychologist, not physical) told me that I should lose the term *victim* from my vocabulary because it would amplify my anger and depression. But now the stroke is too fresh and I'm not ready to be that bold and objective. I am still angry and want to enjoy the rage.

I was working at my job, inspecting auto parts. Yes, I was one of those guys who missed the defective Takata airbags; sue me. I was on the assembly line and had my head bent underneath the dash of a Honda Civic and then the world started to whirl. I could not feel my left side and was aware enough to stumble out of the car and collapse on the ground. My co-worker called 911.

I remember a portly EMS technician with a bulging muffin-top, yelling at me, "What is your name? How many fingers am I holding?"

I knew what she was saying but my words came out slurred and rearranged, like pig Latin. I vaguely recall an intravenous being rammed into the crook of my elbow and being placed on a stretcher. I heard another EMS guy talking on his radio.

When I hit the ER door, it was like a flock of seagulls descending on bread crumbs. One placed an oxygen monitor on my finger, another put oxygen plastic tubes in my nose, and a third wrapped a blood pressure cuff on my arm without the intravenous.

A short Hispanic man poked my arm with another needle for blood. All sorts of voices were shouting orders to unseen people. I caught only bits and pieces, and most of the words were medical sounding and therefore unintelligible to me. They might as well have been speaking Swahili.

"Stat CT without contrast."

"He may be a candidate for thrombolytic therapy or a stent."

"Call neurology and neurosurgery."

"Vital signs are stable. BP 160-90, pulse 90, O_2 sat 93%."

After the CT scan, I was whisked back to the ER where a tall, scruffy doctor approached. He introduced himself, but I don't recall his name. I remember that he had a week old beard and looked like he hadn't slept in days. The bags under his eyes looked like potato sacks.

"Jason, you have suffered an acute stroke affecting the right side of your brain, and therefore the left side of your body. You are lucky since you are right-handed; your speech should improve with time. We believe the cause is a blockage of the carotid artery on the right side of your neck. We have already spoken with your wife, and she has given us permission to administer a clot-busting drug. This should dissolve the clot and restore normal blood flow to your brain in a few minutes. It is generally safe, but sometimes it can cause bleeding in your brain and make the stroke worse. This doesn't happen very often, however."

Wow, I thought. *Lucky me.* I simply nodded my head in consent, not wanting to embarrass myself with garbled attempts at speech.

Within minutes, I felt a small lump move up my right arm and a cool sensation. The clot-dissolving medicine moved swiftly through my vein, then heart, lungs, back to the heart and out the main arteries, including my carotids. Then in a magical instant, I felt the numbness around my mouth and left arm and leg fade. I could wiggle my toes and fingers. I tried to speak.

"I'm feelin' ... uh ... betta ... uh, I think."

The name on Dr. Beard's lab coat said Samuel Moritz. He cracked a smile and said, "Move your fingers and toes, please."

I obeyed and they cooperated. Warm tears began to leak from my eyes.

"Tank you berry much."

"You're welcome. You need to rest now. We will place you on milder blood thinners and keep you for two to three days for further tests and rehab."

I was, of course, grateful. The anger would come later.

The subsequent tests revealed a ninety-five percent blockage of my carotid artery. A heart doctor placed a stent inside of the artery via a tube shoved up my groin artery. I felt nothing. I was placed on blood thinners and after three days sent home to "recover." The word was curious in my condition. I thought of it as being able to regain what had been lost. However, when I came home, I felt like that would never happen. In days, I had gone from active and strong to a cripple. My "self-pity pot" was enormous. I lashed out at Marie for no reason, as well as the dog. Instead of being grateful for help bathing and toileting, I resented my incapacity. Although the strength and sensations in my limbs improved, I still watched my hand and fingers drift like a feather in the air, at times without control.

My neurologist suggested a full recovery was possible but not to get my hopes up too much. He told me depression is common after a stroke and the "happy chemical" in the brain, serotonin, gets depleted after brain damage. He suggested psychotherapy and an antidepressant medication. I accepted the medication offer and declined the shrink.

"I'm sick of being sick," I told my wife only two weeks after my incident. She looked at me with an empathetic but empty stare.

"Patience was never one of your strong points," Marie said. Which now brings me back to Michael Dunbar.

Michael is a squat, pale redhead with freckles. He looks like he just strolled out of a bar in Dublin after consuming one too many Guinness Stouts. He breaks the ice with some self-humor.

"I know what you're thinking," he says. "How can a short, fat guy teach a former Olympic athlete to walk again?"

I just smile.

"Well, here's the thing. I'm not teaching you how to perform track and field events. I'm here to help you *relearn* things you already know. We have to awaken parts of your brain that performed movements automatically before your ..."

"Stroke. Go ahead and say it. I'm getting used to it."

"It's normal to be angry about this. But no one ever got better believing they're a victim. When you get past this, your real rehabilitation will start."

My wife sits quietly in the corner and tries her best not to smirk.

Michael doesn't let up. "Do you think you're the only person to ever have a stroke? If you want to work with me, you'll need to get past the self-pity. How long had you been jumping before you made it to the Olympics?"

"Ten years."

"So then ten months of rehab should seem like nothing to you. And that's about the average time it will take for you to get back seventy-five percent of your strength."

Put that way, it's hard to disagree. I stare at my feet and pout. My weight shifts nervously from one leg to the other. He reaches out with both short arms extended.

"Now grab both of my forearms with your hands."

I do as commanded although my left-hand grip feels weak.

As I reach for his right arm, I watch my hand fall off like a toad jumping off a rolling log. I frown.

"Again," he commands.

And again I grasp his arm and watch mine fall away.

"Fuck!" I exclaim.

"Again."

We do the same exercise another dozen times, until finally he reaches over with his left hand and holds my useless limb steady.

"Why didn't you do that twelve times ago?" I ask.

"Because you need to learn how to accept failure with grace."

"That's just cruel."

About twenty minutes later I am finally able to keep my hand on his forearm without it falling. I feel the smallest sensation in my palm and that allows me to use what little strength remains in my hand.

He smiles and says, "That's enough for today. We'll do more tomorrow."

I am mentally exhausted. Even the smallest of tasks, like eating, getting dressed, and wiping my butt seem too difficult. Luckily Marie is keeping a log of my daily accomplishments, and at the end of two weeks, she shows me my progress.

"Baby steps," she says. Then she shows me what activities of daily living (ADL) I can do now that I could not do two weeks before. I reluctantly agree that progress is being made, albeit too slowly for my liking. Katie returns but senses my resistance to her instructions.

"You can have Michael instead of me. I won't take it personally."

I retain Michael as my therapist and not a day goes by that he isn't pushing me to my limits. There is not a single, "Attaboy" or "Congratulations," uttered. He remains task-oriented and philosophical.

"Nothing good ever came that was easy," he says.

"Socrates?" I ask.

"No. Michael Dunbar," he says with a half-cracked smile.

Days lapse into weeks, and weeks into months. At about four months after my stroke, I am finally able to reach my hand up firmly on his arm, at least until he moves it away, and then it drops like a stone in a pond.

"Hey, that's not fair," I say. "You should have warned me."

"Oh, I'm sorry," he quips. "Perhaps I should tell all the cars in your neighborhood not to move when you approach."

Okay. I get the point.

The thing about recovery from any serious illness is that it's a little like being reborn—not the Christian holy-roller kind, but learning basic stuff all over again. And then there are things that nobody seems to talk about, like sex. My desire is all but gone, until Marie and I meet with my neurologist for my three-month appointment.

"How's your sex life?" he asks.

Marie and I look at each as if we were just asked to solve the formula for nuclear fusion.

"Is that a joke?" I ask.

"No, not at all," he says.

"Is it safe?" Marie asks.

"Yes."

She is tentative and needs more convincing. She looks at the doctor with a quizzical frown.

"You won't cause another stroke or heart attack, if that's what you're thinking," he says.

We both heave a sigh of relief before he throws out a caveat.

"But don't put too much pressure on yourselves. Take your time and try and get back into the saddle slowly. There should not be any rush to 'do it.'"

We get the message and both feel a wave of relief. Before my stroke, we had sex two to three times a week. Not only have we lost the chance for physical release but important marital closeness as well. Now this is progress.

There are voices in my head that won't go away. "Never give up." "Failure is not an option." "Only the strong survive." The clichés go on and on. I remember these things uttered by my workaholic father as a child. He usually wasn't there. For as long as I can remember, he worked two jobs to ensure my Mom could stay home and raise the kids. He was old-fashioned and a relentless disciplinarian. He wouldn't beat us physically, but he did beat us up emotionally. My goal as a teenager was to finally make him say he was proud of me—something he had never done when I was a child. I worked out every day after school at track and field. I ran cross-country, did pole vault and high jumps, and just about anything to gain his attention. When he would attend my track meets, he might utter "good job," or "you're getting better," but never those magical words that I so desperately wanted to hear.

Finally, about the time I made the Olympic trials, he had a heart attack. As he lay dying in the hospital, I came to visit and held his hand. I looked him in the eyes, hidden behind the oxygen mask. I asked, "Are you proud of me, Dad?"

"Yes, son. I am."

Tears poured out of my eyes as I looked at him and said, "I love you." He just nodded his head and drifted back off into a morphine haze. He died that night.

As Michael pushes, I start to feel less sorry for myself. Walking becomes easier. At about four months post-stroke, I give up the cane. I limp a bit but am able to walk the dog by myself and get dressed. One day he arrives at the front door with a yoga mat.

Are we doing Pilates?" I ask.

"No," is all he says. He rolls up the mat, secures it with a black Velcro band, and then lays it at my feet. "Now jump."

I look at him like he has seven heads. "You're kidding, right?"

"No. Jump."

I gaze at the rounded blue log and approach it like a lion stalking its prey. I look at him and then down at the mat. Defiantly, I walk over it and smirk.

"Again," he commands. "But this time jump. I didn't say walk over it."

I stare at the lump on the floor and then crouch a bit. As I launch a few inches off the ground, I lose my balance, and he grabs my arm before I can fall. He then reaches into his back pocket and takes out a wide tan belt with a silver buckle. He straps it around my waist and gets behind me. He grabs a piece of it and says, "Now jump again."

I do as commanded, and before I can fall, he exerts counter pressure and keeps me upright. We do this for fifteen minutes, until I am exhausted.

"Are you trying to embarrass me?"

"No," he says dryly. "I'm trying to get you to jump. But that's enough of this for today."

It takes three more sessions before I can jump over the mat without falling. I looked at it and am discouraged. It cannot be more than four inches high. He finally removes the belt and says, "Now do it by yourself."

I gaze at the blue menace and sigh. Feeling my arms and legs and imagining balance, I jump and landed without falling.

"Tomorrow I'll bring a bigger mat. Next week we'll get to that Amazon box."

I try to smile and he smiles back at me—something he rarely does.

He then gives me a pat on my back and says, "Jason, I am proud of you."

The Lover of Things
and Super Girl

He looked at the polished black hood and chrome and smiled. Then he noticed a small spot he had missed with his microfiber cloth. He grabbed his California Gold Clay Bar wax and went back over it again. Finally, he stuck his head inside the car and used his fine camelhair brush to dust off the AC vents and cup holders. Satisfied that all was well, he stood back with folded arms and admired the cold steel beauty.

Ken Delaney took the driver seat and started the engine. It was only a few yards, but he carefully moved it into his four-car garage and spread out a canvas cover that had fleece on the inside to prevent micro-scratches. His Tesla P90D went from 0-60 mph in 2.8 seconds and had a top speed of 155 mph. He had waited months for the speed upgrade and spent more for it than most people did on a new home. He didn't care. It fit in nicely with his other four cars—the red 2016 Porsche 911 GT3 RS, a white 1995 SL73 AMG Mercedes Benz, and a brand new copper colored Lexus LX SUV.

All were in mint condition and he looked over the lot of them like fine Arabian thoroughbreds or a harem. One of his ex-girlfriends, Alexandria, had half-joked with him that "he loved his cars more than her, and if he could have sex with them, he would." He had smiled when she said that, for it was indeed true.

With all of his money and other big boy "toys," it was easy to imagine him buying and selling autos frequently. But in fact, it was hard for him to part with them. He more easily exchanged women than he did cars, and was clearly more attached to the machines. His heart ached when he would decide to sell one, or Lord forbid, he scratched or dented one. Not that he needed to sell one anyway. He had more money than 1,000 people make in a lifetime. He had accumulated his wealth at first by owning dozens of storage units that, after the mortgages were paid off, were cash cows. Then at the bottom of the real estate market in 2009, he bought up gobs of foreclosed properties in gorgeous areas of Florida, Arizona, and California. For several years he sat on his losses until the market roared back, and then he just flipped properties. He sheltered all of his earnings in a foundation for foster children and threw regular banquets and raised more cash from wealthy donors.

His foundation, For the Children, served three purposes:

tax sheltering of his fortune, bolstering his public image of a being more altruistic than greedy, and a great way to meet women. As the top eligible bachelor in Hollywood, Florida, he went through girlfriends like a dog went through chew toys. He was having too much fun to ever consider getting married and having a family, even as he approached his fortieth birthday. Although an introvert, he forced himself to have fundraising banquets several times a year and played the magnanimous philanthropist role well. To qualify for his foundation, he had a small number of faithful, and well-paid, employees who searched out homeless families with children, single mothers with multiple kids, and sick children with little or no health insurance. He had a dynamic website and at the banquets showed tear-jerking videos of the new beneficiaries of his largesse. He would donate heavily to silent auctions, along with other wealthy friends and businesses, creating all-expense paid trips to the Florida Keys or Disney World. A compulsive planner and master of control, he was totally unprepared for the day his world would change.

It was a sunny, crisp day in March as he left his mansion on an open-water canal. Although Ken deplored going to malls or stores, he ventured out to a local jewelry store to buy a special gift for his latest girlfriend, Kim Mullins. He walked out of the store quickly with a floppy fishing hat pulled down over his brow, hoping not to be recognized.

At first he did not see the long wooden table set up with

several little girls in brown uniforms hawking Girl Scout cookies.

"Excuse me, sir, but you look like someone who would really like to buy some Thin Mints."

At first he said nothing and looked around to see if the little street urchin was speaking to someone else.

"Excuse me?" he asked.

"Thin Mints—you know, those chocolate minty cookies that no one can resist," she said boldly upping her sales pitch. "I am sure you ate them when you were younger. Perhaps your sister sold them?"

"No. I was an only child."

"Didn't your mom buy them for you?" Ken thought for a moment. The child was relentless.

"What's your name?"

"Rebecca. Rebecca Morrison."

"Well, Rebecca Morrison, you are quite a salesperson. How many boxes do you have?"

"I'm not sure. Wait a minute please." She conferred with her scout leader, an overweight woman with drab brown hair and an overflowing waist.

"Thirty," she responded with a wide smile.

"Well then, I will take them all."

"Really?" Rebecca said, stunned.

"Yes, really."

"Wow.... that's super. Let me get you a big box."

"How much?" Ken asked.

The scrawny child punched in some numbers on an old calculator and said, "$150."

Ken reached for his wallet and pulled out three crisp $50 bills.

The little girl stared at the bills with wide eyes. He watched her long, sausage curled, brown hair dangling on her shoulders and could not help but think of Little Orphan Annie.

She reached for the cash and placed them into a well-worn open cigar box that sat on top of the frayed folding table. She assembled the boxes and stacked them up five high and in six neat columns.

She hesitated and then said, "Can I ask you something?"

"Sure."

Dead serious, she cocked her head to the side and said, "How are you going to eat all of those cookies?"

Ken at first smiled and then let out a huge belly laugh that drew the attention of the other scouts, their leader, and passers-bys. Tears started to well up in his eyes but then saw the embarrassment on her face as she blushed, thinking she must have just asked the dumbest question in the world. Her hurt and pain was obvious and Ken sensed an emotion that was foreign to him—regret, regret over his laughter.

"I'm sorry," he said. "Your question wasn't stupid. I just imagined myself eating them and it gave me a funny picture of stuffing my mouth full with chocolate oozing around my lips."

That helped to curb Rebecca's humiliation and she cracked a smile. Before she could ask the obvious next question, her wealthy buyer answered it for her.

"You see, Rebecca, I have a big company with a lot of employees. I'm sure I will have no trouble giving them out as gifts."

That made Rebecca even happier. She just stared at him and continued to smile.

Ken reached out his arm and gave her a firm handshake.

"I hope you sell a lot more cookies today."

"Thank you," was all she said.

"I will drive my car around and load them up. Could you give me a hand?"

She nodded her head with enthusiasm and Ken watched as her long curls danced upon her shoulders.

He drove his Mercedes AMG around and she helped load the boxes into the back seat. He could tell she wanted to ask him something else.

"Yes?" he asked.

She hesitated and then said, "Wow. I've never seen a car like this before."

"Really?" he asked, but already knew she was telling the truth.

"Do you want to go for a ride in it?"

Her entire face lit up and he saw a smile so broad he thought her cheeks would crack.

"Really? I will have to ask Mrs. Cromwell for permission."

He glanced over at the scout leader and approached her with self-confidence. After introducing himself and shaking hands, she blushed and appeared to be in some shock.

"You are THE Ken Delaney?"

"Yes, I am." He then proffered her a business card from his wallet.

"I see," the leader said. "I can't let her go off now. It wouldn't look good for the other girls. I'm sure you understand."

"Of course," he said. "How about another time?"

"I think we could arrange that, yes."

She gave him her phone number and asked him to call later.

Ken nodded and then told Rebecca the expensive ride would not happen today but sometime soon. Although he saw some disappointment register on her face, she shrugged her shoulders and simply said, "Okay."

Ken walked away with a warm glow deep inside. It was a different kind of feeling from one he had ever had, even after buying a new toy or making another sexual conquest. It felt new because it was. He had never felt so good about offering something before without the promise of anything in return.

A week later he had arranged to pick up Rebecca at her foster home. He found out that Mrs. Cromwell was in fact her foster mother, and that Rebecca and her siblings had been abused as children by her alcoholic parents. Child welfare had placed them into various foster homes around the state. Indeed, in her eleven young years, she was now on her fourth family. Rebecca had scored high in standardized testing and was doing well in school. However, she had a deep distrust of any adult. Thus, it had surprised Mrs. Cromwell that she seemed so open and friendly with Ken Delaney.

Standing in his garage, Ken could not decide which of his trophy cars to take out. He felt like he was about to go on the most important date of his life and this realization shocked and mystified him. Finally, he decided on the least ostentatious—his Lexus SUV.

When he arrived at her foster home, it was in a lower middle-class neighborhood. The white stucco bungalow-style house was in some disrepair with peeling paint and pitted wood but seemed clean. The ordinary Florida landscape of pampas grass, bromeliads, and old oak trees was interrupted with yards of dollar weed poking through what little grass had survived neglect. It was a far cry from the manicured lawns and yards he had grown used to seeing in his neighborhood. When he rang the front bell, Mrs. Cromwell came to the door with a plain white blouse, an eyelet skirt, flip flops and an apron. Her hair was parted in the front with a pink ribbon. She looked like a portly southern trailer park version of June Cleaver.

"She'll be out in a minute. Now remember, she hasn't been exposed to much in the world other than playgrounds, Mac-Donald's, and an occasional movie. We shop at Goodwill, The Salvation Army, and the Family Dollar store."

He tried to read the intent of her words but stumbled badly in his response.

"Well, I'm sure we won't be going to any of these places."

The woman just smiled and was diplomatic in her response.

"Of course not. I was just saying this to let you know she'll be in awe of pretty much anything you show or buy her."

He nodded his head. Looking behind her as Rebecca appeared. She was beaming and had on a clean, beige blouse that looked a couple of sizes too big and shorts. A pair of old tatty white sneakers completed her outfit. She had a big smile.

"Okay," said Ken. "Let's go."

He had never wanted for anything as a child. His parents were lawyers, one corporate and the other estate planning. He had grown up in their wealthy Shaker Heights suburb of Cleveland, Ohio, but moved to Ft. Lauderdale when he was twelve. His only encounter with adversity was when his dog, Bongo, a border collie, died while he was in high school. He was never very good at sports but excelled in academics and politics. He was class president and was always in the social spotlight. Yes, Ken Delaney was a lucky child. He graduated second in his class and easily entered Duke University, where he went on to earn degrees in both business and marketing. To him, failure at anything was an anathema.

"So where would you like to go?" Ken asked her.

She could not take her eyes off of the plush leather seats and the twelve inch navigation system on the dashboard.

"I don't know. You mean I get to choose?" she asked.

"Yes."

She bit her lip for a moment and stared out the window as cars flew by on I-95. Although the sun was bright, she did not have to squint because of the heavily tinted bronze glass.

"What are my choices?"

"Movies, pizza parlor, ice cream, or the zoo."

"Movies," she said quickly. "And then maybe ice cream?"

"Sure." Ken pulled over to the side of road and tapped open his Android phone, searching for movies.

"What kind of movies do you like?"

"I don't know. I've never been."

"But Mrs. Cromwell said you have seen movies before."

"All I have seen are some old Disney films on videotapes at the home."

"Hmm," he said, eyes staring at the small screen and scrolling through what was now playing at the theaters.

"How about *Zootopia*?"

"Are there animals in it?" she asked.

"Yes."

"Super. Well, if it has animals, then I will probably like it."

As they walked into the theater, Rebecca's head looked like it was on a swivel. The flashing lights held her gaze and the smell of popcorn and butter flooded her nostrils. Her senses were overwhelmed and perceiving she was confused by all of the lights and music, he took her hand in his as they paid for the tickets and walked into the theater.

"What would you like to eat?" he asked as they approached the counter. She looked at the array of Twizzlers, Sour Tarts, and candy bars and just stared blankly.

"How about some popcorn?" he prompted. "Have you ever had any before?"

She just shook her head and said, "Kind of...I mean I had some made in a microwave oven."

Ken laughed and said, "Oh my honey, this will be much better."

"One large bucket of popcorn with butter please," he said leaning on the glass counter.

"Anything to drink?" asked the pimple-faced young man standing on the other side with a drab brown theater chain uniform.

"Hmmm, I'll have a bottle of water and she'll have a regular small Coke."

As they settled into their stadium-style leather seats, Ken could tell that, although she was excited, Rebecca kept an invisible emotional fence around her. It was nothing obvious, but he could sense that her distance was protective, perhaps born out of past traumas or disappointments in her short life. He took a cue and tried not to invade her space. He was cautious and asked first before he acted or said anything.

"Would you like some popcorn?" He asked before the movie started. He could see her hesitate and then said, "Oh shoot, I should have gotten you your own bucket; maybe you don't want to share it with me?"

She thought for a moment and then said, "No, that's okay. I don't think I have any cooties."

Ken laughed and said, "Me either."

With the ice broken her hand dove into the bucket like she was eating her last meal. Ken had only a few handfuls, just to be polite. As the movie started, he could not help staring at her. Her eyes were transfixed on the large screen and ears attentive to the Dolby Surround Sound system. He was not a big fan of cartoons, but he did, however, find himself becoming engrossed in the story. It seemed like it was over in a few minutes. As they left the theater, he asked, "Do you still want ice cream?"

"Sure."

They drove to a locally owned ice cream store and she ordered a hot fudge sundae with whipped cream. She devoured it in minutes. Ken was incredulous.

"Where do you put all of this food? It's like you haven't eaten in weeks."

She replied dryly, "I put it in my stomach. Where else did you think it would go?" They both laughed.

As they left the ice cream parlor, the heavens opened up with a typical Florida afternoon thunderstorm. They ran to the car, both soaked but giggling and happy. As Ken drove her home he reflected on how quickly the day had gone and how happy he felt. All of his life had been devoted to making only one person happy—himself. He only now began to feel that perhaps all of this self-absorption was for naught. It seemed trivial and silly. He thought of himself as bright. But the obvious lack of true benevolence that had become the cornerstone of his life and the emotional void it produced, stunned him. It was nothing short of an epiphany, in fact. How childish and self-centered he had been and how many years he had wasted, he thought.

He pulled out a large umbrella as the rain was letting up. He walked her to the door and rang the bell. Before an adult could answer he said, "I had a great time today. I hope you did too. Perhaps we can do it again?"

"Super," was all she said.

It did not take long before most of Rebecca's free time out of school was spent with Ken. They bonded like soul mates. Ken spent less time with his several girlfriends and more time with his new one. He called her "Super Girl" because every time they went out and he asked her about her time with him, she would answer with one word only...*super*.

He began to feel like a Disney Dad. They went to aquariums, theme parks, miniature golf, and pizza parlors. After a few weeks, he could tell that perhaps she was tiring of all of the special treatment. After one of their outings, he asked her, "Are you happy?"

"Yes," she answered. "Super happy. How about you?"

"Super-super happy."

Before long Ken started to entertain her at his home. He was self-conscious at first letting her see the size and opulence of his residence. She stood gaping-mouth at his dock, staring at his 48-foot Hatteras yacht. They would devour take-home pizza, tacos, and barbeque chicken. She even acquired a taste for Thai food. Then they would settle into the large leather reclining seats of his home theater and watch one movie after another, like *Finding Nemo*, *Toy Story*, and *Up*. But her favorite one wasn't a cartoon. It was *Annie*. She watched it over and over again. Ken wasn't sure why because after each viewing she seemed sad. One day after the closing credits she asked him, "Would you ever adopt me?"

He did not remember the date or time she asked this, but later recalled it was a Wednesday night. He was stunned and, for one of the first times in his life, wordless. After stuttering and stumbling badly for a few seconds, she withdrew the question.

"It's okay. I shouldn't have asked you that," she said biting her lip.

"It's okay honey. It's just that's a very complicated and grown-up question."

The couple's usual high spirits seemed muted after that and Rebecca sensed that she had crossed a delicate line.

The next Friday morning, Kim Mullins walked into Ken's stainless steel and marble kitchen wearing a white cotton bathrobe. Her perfect size breasts peaked out, creating an inviting valley. She still smelled of sex. Ken was drinking at the counter while reading some papers online with his tablet perched at a 45-degree angle on top of the sugar jar.

"Want some coffee?" he asked.

"Sure."

He poured her a cup and added some cream and exactly one teaspoon of sugar, as he knew she liked.

"Something on your mind?" he asked, raising his eyes a little bit over his reading glasses.

"Yeah, sort of, I guess. I was just wondering if your other girlfriend was coming over tonight?"

Ken started to bite his lip softly and stared at her eyes, almost boring through her skull, but at the same time appearing concerned and sympathetic.

"By my other girlfriend, are you referring to Rebecca?"

Kim nodded as she sipped her coffee. "Sometimes I think you love her more than me."

"Oh sweetie, do you think I am a child molester?"

"No, it's just that you seem so much happier when she is around."

Ken decided to handle the jealous innuendo with diplomacy. "I just love her in a different way than I love you, that's all." Kim seemed mollified, at least for the moment.

"I suppose not having children of your own makes you yearn for that relationship."

"Yes," he said, "and I have never felt so fulfilled in my life treating her to things that she never had. Besides, some day, when you have children, you might see how that love is different too. "

She nodded. Being only twenty-two years old and starting a career as a paralegal during the day and going to law school at night did not give her much time for developing a family, not that Ken was the marrying or fathering type. She was certain of this and harbored no illusions. However, every girlfriend he had acquired fancied herself as The One who would change all that and drive him to a commitment.

"Anyway, I will be late for work if I don't get going. Call me."

"I will."

She waltzed away towards the bedroom and, after a few feet, allowed her robe to drop to the floor. Her slim waist and bouncy hips revealed a string bikini tan line and as she tossed her long, blonde hair over her shoulders. She looked back at her lover. "And make sure it's soon."

Ken laughed and saw dimples appear at the corners of her mouth. Her blue eyes dazzled and he felt like he could take her again right there on the counter.

After several months, during her non-school hours, it seemed that Rebecca was always with Ken. He took her boating and taught her to boogie board in the waves at Hollywood Beach. She began to experience fine food and went to fancy car meetings with him as well.

In May, he took her to see Disney's *Frozen on Ice*, at the BB&T Center in Sunrise, where the Florida Panthers hockey team played. She had never seen ice before, other than inside of a soda glass, and having spent her whole short life in South Florida, rarely experienced cold weather. Ken was aware of what she might feel and bought her a Florida Panthers sweater at the team store before the performance started. As they walked down to their seats, she clutched a pink cotton candy cone. Her eyes widened as she tried to take in the smell of fresh ice and the dazzling warm-up light show. She watched intently as the Zamboni truck glided over the ice surface.

"What is that thing?" she asked.

"It's a special truck that makes the ice smooth and easier for the skaters to skate on," Ken replied.

"It looks cool. Can anyone ride on it?"

"Not just anyone," he said, hiding a smile.

"Oh," was all she said.

She sat huddled up to him as the show started with multi-colored lights bouncing off of the ice, singing, and music. She was in a trance. She had long ago let Ken cross her touching boundary and cuddled up to him. She sat spellbound in her leather seat, turning her head from side to side as the performers raced past. Being in the fifth row from the ice, she could hear the skate blades digging into the frozen surface as the skaters twirled and jumped.

At intermission, she asked for a Carvel hot fudge sundae but didn't finish it. This was unusual as her appetite for junk food was insatiable.

"Are you okay?" Ken asked.

"Yes," she answered. "Just a little bit tired."

"Well, you need to get some energy back because I have a surprise for you."

Her eyes lit up as he grabbed her hand. They walked down to the ice level and past a security guard as Ken flashed some credentials. After a short walk, they came upon a large, heavy, navy-colored felt curtain. Ken drew it aside. Before her stood the large Zamboni with a stepladder.

"Okay, Princess," he said. "It's time for your ride."

"No way!" she exclaimed.

"Yes, but that's not all." He pointed to the curtain as Elsa and Anna actresses appeared in twinkling dresses and robes.

"Oh my God!" Rebecca howled.

"Hello, Rebecca," Elsa said. "May we ride with you?"

She could not find any words and only nodded up and down like a bobble head doll.

As the three of them climbed on board, the driver hit the pedal and they rode out onto the ice. The lights were dazzling, almost blinding, and she just beamed as the actresses and she waved to a hooting and cheering crowd. In ten minutes the ride was over, but Rebecca felt like it had lasted an hour. As Ken helped her down, he asked her, "Well, how was it?"

"Super times three!" was all she could say.

As they sat and watched the second act, Ken could sense that something was wrong. Rebecca could hardly keep her eyes open. He looked at her and she seemed pale and withdrawn. At the finale, she did not stand up to cheer or applaud. He became increasingly worried and started to ask her, "Honey are you...?" But before he could finish his question she wretched up a massive amount of blood as red streams poured out her nostrils.

"Somebody call 911!" he screamed. He caught her as she began to fall and lose consciousness. Warm red liquid filled his hands.

He sat still inside the ambulance as the paramedics established an IV and gave her oxygen. Rebecca's color was pasty white, and her *Frozen* sweater was now covered in dry and gelatinous blobs of dark red blood. He had his hands entwined and propped up on his knees as he listened in horror to the emergency that was still unfolding.

"Base, this is American Ambulance Unit 33. We have a child in hemorrhagic shock with a BP of 60/30 and a pulse of 130. We are requesting authorization from Joe DiMaggio Children's Hospital for expedited ER care."

"Affirmative 33, we will take care of this. Let me patch you through to their facility now."

Ken held his breath for what like seemed an hour but in actuality was probably only a couple of minutes. He felt numb as his thoughts swirled out of control. He was worried that it had been his fault—too many sweets or excitement. Then the more rational part of his mind took over and identified these musings as ridiculous.

"JD ER here," squawked the husky female voice on the other end of the two-way radio. "With whom am I speaking?"

"This is EMS Unit 33. We are on our way to your facility with a young girl, about eleven or twelve years old, who is bleeding and in shock. The source appears to be internal without outer signs of obvious trauma. Her male friend says he is unaware of any history of chronic illnesses or whether she had been sick. And she hasn't been complaining of anything"

The ER woman hesitated a moment and asked, "Her male friend? How old is he?"

"About forty. He says he is her friend and had taken her out for the day to the Disney ice show."

Although the ER operator did not comment further, Ken knew how bad this sounded. In this age of pedophilia, an older man just didn't take a young girl out for the day unless he was a relative. He would deal with that later.

"We will get several units of packed red cells, type O ready, and platelets. What is your ETA?"

"Five to ten minutes," the ambulance driver said.

"Okay, see you shortly. Over."

"Over and out."

Again the few minutes felt like hours, but as soon as the flashing and siren screaming truck pulled up to the ER entrance, medical staff descended upon the van like locusts. Ken sat aside and gratefully watched the experienced crew do their stuff. As Rebecca was whisked into the cold, sterile bowels of the hospital, he got out and walked into the admitting area. He approached an older woman with an ID badge around her neck, seated in front of the computer.

She looked up over her reading glasses and asked, "May I help you?"

"Uh, yes. I just arrived with a girl in an ambulance. She's bleeding and quite sick. I wanted to give my name and make sure you know I can pay for everything involved with her care."

This, of course, gave the admitting clerk pause, since most of her clients were trying to get out of their bills, had fake insurance, or get someone else to pay for them. Ken steeled himself for the inevitable question.

"And what may I ask is your relationship to the girl?"

"I am a friend."

"Then I can't let you register her or give you any information about her condition without parental consent," the woman sad coldly.

"But she doesn't have any parents. I mean she is in a foster home."

"That doesn't matter. If you aren't her parent or family, or have power of attorney, you are just someone off the street to me."

Not one used to being told he couldn't do something, the hairs on his neck bristled and his jaw squared. Then he realized with all of the panic and commotion he had not even called Mrs. Cromwell.

"I understand. If I can reach her foster mom and she gives you permission by phone would that help?"

"Perhaps, yes," was the only thing the stern woman said.

"Ok, please give me a moment." He tapped on his smart phone and dialed Patty Cromwell's phone number praying she would answer. The older woman with the loose, wrinkled tan skin just stared at him.

On the sixth ring, she said, "Hello?"

"Patty, this is Ken. I am afraid I have some rather bad news." He proceeded to describe the events of the day and could hear the older woman sobbing.

"But I don't have a car right now and have other kids at home. I can't leave and come to the hospital," she said.

"That's all right, " said Ken. "Let me try something else. Stay on the line.

With that he handed the phone to the clerk and heard her ask some brief questions. She must have been on the phone for less than one minute when she handed the phone back to Ken.

"She says I have to come in with proof of parental authority before she will speak with either of us about Becky's condition."

Ken could feel his face redden and the heat rising under his collar. Before he could say anything, Patty spoke up.

"I think I can get a neighbor to watch the kids for a while. Can you come and get me?"

"Yes," he said.

And with that Ken told the clerk he would return shortly. He raced out of the hospital to his car and drove rapidly to the home, running several red lights along the way. He prayed he wouldn't be stopped. By the time he got to the foster home, Patty was dressed and ready to go, with documentation papers in hand. As he drove back he tried to elaborate more on the events. Patty added some more recent history.

"She did seem a bit listless the past few days and had no appetite. It's not like her at all as you know. In fact, I was going to take her to the doctor next week if she didn't perk up."

As Patty spoke, he just nodded his head and looked straight ahead, fearing the worse.

Clearing all of the privacy hurdles and signing a few ridiculous paper forms at the ER registration desk, they were finally able to speak with the ER doctor. He was a short, somewhat disheveled Middle Eastern man with a dark week-old beard and jet black hair. He introduced himself as Dr. Al-Hazan. Ken immediately wondered if he was secretly a terrorist and then quickly re-focused his attention. His English was passable but with a heavy accent.

"She has been moved to the Pediatric ICU. She is very ill. Her hemoglobin is only five and we will be transfusing her shortly."

"What is normal?" Ken asked.

"11 to 13, so hers is less than half of that. Her blood count also shows markedly depressed white blood cell and platelet counts. There are many things that can cause this, but I am worried this might be leukemia."

He felt as if a piano had been dropped on his head.

"Are you serious?" he asked. He was aware of Patty starting to tear up and sob.

"Yes, I am afraid so. There are, of course, other more benign things, like infections. But right now that is our working diagnosis. A blood specialist will be seeing her later today. I am very sorry."

He had hundreds of questions but knew he was being handed off to another set of specialists and thanked the doctor. After being given directions to the ICU, Ken took Patty's hand and walked down the sterile hallway towards an elevator. Neither one said anything.

The smell of antiseptic spray and soaps hit his nose before

they rang the bell to the ICU. After identifying them, a young Filipino nurse escorted the pair to Rebecca's room. The reality of her condition caused Patty's soft sobs to break into loud crying. Ken wrapped his arm around her shoulder and felt as if it the dam holding his tears might burst as well. Rebecca had tubes everywhere: from her mouth, her nose, her arms, and her urethra.

"Is she awake?" he asked.

"No," said the nurse. "She's sedated. I can't tell you what to do or what will happen, but why don't you consider going home, getting something to eat and rest? Then you can come back in a few hours."

Patty looked at Ken and they both knew the answer.

"No," was all Patty said. "We'll take turns staying here." She then pivoted to Ken and said, "I've got the next few hours covered. Why don't you go home and come back at seven and relieve me?"

Ken nodded. He gathered his unfeeling body and walked out of the ICU, still in utter disbelief.

He stood for a long time in his marble and glass shower. As the fat droplets of water careened off his head from his extra-large rainforest showerhead, he just stared as soap and water escaped down the drain. He lost track of time but finally grabbed his Egyptian cotton "bath mat" towel and dried off. With his towel wrapped around his waist he walked into his living room that looked out onto the intra-coastal waterway through floor-to-ceiling soft-tinted glass. The sun was almost gone. He could not shake his numbness, and even urgent text and voicemail messages from Kim could not brighten his mood. He left them unanswered.

He went behind his wet bar and grabbed a tall bottle of Chopin vodka. He was not much of a drinker, feeling that doing so left him vulnerable and out of control. He saved it mostly for female guests who seemed to require it before foreplay and jumping into his bed. Today, however, he didn't care. He mixed himself a tall Baccarat glass of vodka, Cointreau, and POM pomegranate juice. Any illusions he had harbored about control were now gone. He had controlled his businesses, his workers, and he thought even his lovers. But now that he had found someone to love in a different way, and that control was being wrested from him. It was as if God, or a higher power, was saying to him, *See? You think you can control everything, but in reality you control nothing.*

The diagnosis of leukemia was especially painful, as his best friend from college had died of it. He knew full well what the odds were and what the script would be over the next few months. There would be chemotherapy, drug trials, maybe radiation, and even a bone marrow transplant if all else failed. He would pay for all of this and find her the finest doctors and medical centers money could buy. But since his friend had died at MD Anderson in Houston, and it was one of the best, he knew there were no guarantees. Super Girl had met her match.

The future was uncertain. All he could think about was how unimportant all of his prior relationships and love of inanimate objects had been. They had not brought him happiness. Only Rebecca had done that. And now her future was hanging by the thinnest of threads.

Dark

She had never felt so alone. The air was pressing down and it was hard to breathe. Nothing in the room was familiar. It smelled medicinal and the heat was oppressive. At first she thought she might die, and then she wanted to die—anything to make all of this go away.

"Alice," the voice said. "Can you hear me?"

She nodded her head.

"Can you speak?"

She could but she was afraid to and so shook her head from side to side. Her brunette hair danced over a wet brow. Her lips were dry, cracked, and tasted like salt. Her vision was fuzzy.

"Okay, then," the voice said. "Do you know where you are?"

Again, she shook her head. She wanted to scream but

couldn't. She could not recall anything about why she was in such an awful place.

"Okay. Let me try to orient you. You had an overdose. Your boyfriend found you and called 911. You were given medication to reverse the drugs, and that is when you started fighting with the EMS team. They had to restrain and sedate you. Do you remember any of this?"

Again, she shook her head and for the first time realized that she was tied down. Cloth and leather restraints pushed against her wrists and ankles. A soft vest was pulled tightly over her breasts. She felt like a mummy. She started to cry but had no tears. Her throat was dry and parched. She looked over at her left side and saw intravenous tubing and read the plastic bag—D5NS0.9%. *It should be going faster*, she thought. But wait, how did she know that? Only then did she remember she was a nurse.

Her boyfriend? She did not remember having a boyfriend. Her thoughts were skittish and the more she tried to remember, the more frustrated she became. She could only focus on her own discomfort and the smells. The air reeked of iodine and bleach. The heart monitor beeped in syncopated rhythm. The sounds became like Chinese water torture—*drip, drip, drip.*

"We are going to have to do an internal female exam," another voice said. She wanted to ask why but couldn't.

Her legs were spread apart and a cold speculum was inserted into her vagina. She squirmed and gasped. Another voice said, "Hand me the rape kit, please."

Finally the assault ended and she was left with the sights, sounds, and smells of an all too familiar place, a hospital. Or at least it felt like a hospital. By the time she found her voice, there was no one in the room to hear her.

"Hey…hey," she hoarsely whispered. She tried to increase the volume but her vocal cords lacked power. Her restraints had been loosened and she found a call bell. After pressing it several times a short, Asian nurse came in.

"May I help you?"

"Yes," she half whispered. "Where am I?"

The nurse said, "I will be right back."

She wanted to scream "Wait!" but could not muster the vocal strength.

It seemed like hours but was probably less. The diminutive nurse came back in with two men in white lab coats. She assumed they were doctors, but her vision was still fuzzy as dirty eyeglasses. She summoned all her strength and tried to focus.

"Where am I and what happened to me?"

The lab coat men stared at each other. The dark-skinned one began to speak. His accent was heavily Indian.

"You were attacked and raped. You took or were given an overdose of narcotics. You were unconscious. You are in Memorial Hospital."

"Who did this to me?"

"We don't know yet. The police are investigating."

Her head throbbed and eyes ached. Her entire body was sore. Between her legs she felt a burning.

"Why can't I see?"

"Your vision will come back. All of your scans and tests point to a full recovery. However, you've suffered a concussion and your thinking and mood may not be normal for a while. You have amnesia."

"How long is a while?"

White coats again looked at each other and this time the taller, skinnier one spoke.

"It's too soon to tell. It could just be days, but we can't rule out weeks or even months."

They left her with the tortuous clicks and beeps of her monitoring machinery. Her skin felt heavy and every bone and joint ached. If black holes existed, then surely she must have fallen inside of one. She felt like screaming and then crying.

She smelled him before she felt or saw him. It was Bay Rum Lime, and it was repulsive. First, there was a hand on her arm. She looked up and saw a short man with cropped brown hair and a day-old beard. He, too, wore a white lab coat but appeared unkempt. As he bent to say something in her ear, a shudder came over her.

"Next time, I will kill you," he said.

Then he left the room.

She hoped it had been just a nightmare but felt too dazed and groggy to know for sure. Reality and dreams were becoming more difficult to distinguish. Nurses came and went. They cleaned her bottom and tried to feed her baby food that she found revolting. She swallowed only to make them happy. As the days progressed, she was able to speak better and started to get out of bed with assistance. At first when she stood, she was dizzy and almost fell. But therapists helped her walk down the hall, and even though at first her legs felt like sponges, they grew stronger. They moved her out of the ICU and to a regular room with a roommate. Her name was Margaret and she was about seventy years old. She had long, stringy, gray hair and looked closer to ninety. She had suffered a heart attack and a small stroke but was mentally sharp and quite talkative.

"So sweetie," Margaret asked. "What are you in here for?" It sounded like a question posed from one prisoner to another.

Alice hesitated and then said, "I was beaten and attacked."

"Oh my," Margaret answered. "I'm so sorry. Did you know him?"

"Know who?"

"Your attacker, of course."

"I know it sounds stupid but I'm not sure. They say I have amnesia."

"Well, I'm sure it will come to you."

Her roommate returned to doing some needlepoint. Her long gray hair fell over the pillow in her lap. She continued to talk.

"Do you have any family?"

"I'm not sure," Alice answered. She began to fidget with her IV dressing. "I feel so stupid."

Looking up from her hobby the elderly woman said, "Oh, don't worry about that. I'm sure it will all come back to you. I can't even remember why I came into a room anymore, and that's not likely to improve."

Alice smiled.

Soon Alice was floating off to sleep and was awakened by the clanging of a stretcher. Her roommate was being wheeled out the door for an x-ray. She felt alone and vulnerable. The blinds over her window were half opened and the late afternoon sun filtered in with dust particles dancing in the light. She stood up and viewed the Seattle skyline and a sliver of gray Puget Sound. The TV was playing a commercial for kitty litter and she remembered she had a cat, Oscar, an old tomcat. She wondered who was taking care of him. She then drifted back into a deep slumber.

A sweaty hand was over her mouth. She could not scream. The smell of Bay Rum Lime struck her nostrils and she began to shake. He leaned over her and whispered in her ear.

"You never should have dumped me. We were good together. All I wanted was for you to love me. But you wouldn't. I didn't have a choice you know. But we can start over again."

His clammy hand reached under her hospital gown and fondled her right breast, and she began to tremble. His hand then moved down her belly to her legs and a finger entered her. He began to roughly massage her as he moaned. She felt like her head might explode. While he was distracted with his other hand buried deep inside her, she bit the fingers covering her lips.

"Ouch! Bitch!" He took his invading hand out of her and slapped her hard across the mouth. She could taste the coppery blood start to ooze and felt like she might faint. Still, she grabbed the telephone handset from her nightstand and slammed his bleeding hand. He howled even louder. Instead of striking her again, he coddled his bleeding hand under his armpit and ran out of the room, the white lab coat flying behind him.

The charge nurse and nursing supervisor stood next to her bed as she repeated the story over and over again. She'd had stitches in her lip and a tetanus shot. The charge nurse was dark-skinned and Alice thought she looked familiar. But all she could recognize was another floor nurse, probably from the Philippines, like dozens of others. The nursing supervisor was middle-aged, slim, and looked younger than her probable age thanks to the miracles of plastic surgery. However, Alice could not take her eyes off the large diamond on her finger.

"Did you catch him?" she asked.

The older nurse, whose face looked like a quilt from her surgeries, shook her head. "No. I'm afraid not. However, we are going over the videos and have some leads."

"Does he work here?" Alice asked.

The nurses exchanged quizzical looks and the supervisor said, "We'd rather not say at this time."

Alice was dumbstruck. "I'm attacked inside your hospital, not only once, but maybe twice, and you'd rather not say? What the hell is going on here?"

The plastic surgery nurse said, "It's complicated. There are some potential legal issues."

"Then I want a lawyer. This is bullshit."

"Your choice."

"And oh, by the way, I may sue your hospital, too," she said through numb and throbbing lips.

"I don't think you want to do that, Alice. However, I will get someone from the Risk Management Department to meet with you. For now, we are giving you a private room and a 24-hour-a-day sitter."

She asked her nurse for a Xanax and drifted off to sleep.

She was in a deep hole, like an abandoned well or mine shaft. It was cold, damp, and she was naked. She clutched her arms around her breasts and waist and shivered uncontrollably. She tried to gain a purchase on some stones jutting out of the wall. She made it a few feet up when a wet hand grabbed her ankle and dragged her to the cold mud. She landed with a *thud* and woke screaming.

A hand rested on her forearm. It felt warm, soft, and kind… not threatening. She was still screaming and shaking.

"Alice, you're okay," a voice said.

A short blonde woman in a gray flannel pantsuit smiled at her.

"Who are you?" Alice asked.

"Cheryl King, Risk Management Department."

Alice squinted at her through wet and crusted eyes. She looked like she was fifteen years old.

"How old are you?"

Blondie smiled and said, "Twenty-two; I know I look young for my age."

"Why are you here?"

"Anybody who is attacked in the hospital deserves a visit from us. We need to assure you we are doing everything possible to catch this man."

"Yeah, and I will be running for President next week," she said.

"I understand why you are upset."

"Why does everyone keep saying that to me? It can't be that hard to catch a madman abusing a woman inside a hospital. Does TSA run your security here?"

Cheryl scrunched her face. "If I were in your place, I would be angry as well. Let me just say we have some leads and I expect a break very soon."

When Alice awoke, her head still seemed in a fog. She looked at her legs and realized she hadn't shaved them in over a week. The stubble stuck out like grass on a putting green. She heard buzzing at the nursing station outside in the hall. It was nighttime and the graveyard shift had checked in for work. Listening to their loud laughter, it evoked a memory of her early days in nursing. She would work nights. They would play cards, tell jokes, and eat donuts. Patients were usually asleep and phones mostly silent. It was a lonely time for her. She had just broken up with her boyfriend—why couldn't she remember his name? Then she met Josh. Josh, the night shift respiratory therapist. He was short with curly hair and always running around the gloomy halls of the hospital in his stupid white lab coat, pretending to be a doctor. Then it struck her hard. It was as if a boulder had fallen on her head. They had dated for a couple of months. It was a tumultuous relationship, on and off again. There were lots of fights, drinking, rough sex, and finally she'd had enough. She moved out of his apartment. Was it only a month ago? As she'd left one murky night, he'd said, "If you leave me I will kill you and myself."

The details and the memories flooded in. His parents had abused him as a child. He spent time in a foster home until a wealthy childless couple adopted him. The adoptive mother stayed at home and played tennis and donated time at The Children's Home. She drove a Mercedes. His father was the CEO of a hospital. Which one? She strained as the memories started to fade. Could it be this one? Could it be that the staff already knew he had attacked her but could not reveal or arrest him for fear of parental retribution? She sat alone in the bed. Her television was muted as infomercials played on in an endless loop. She had never felt so utterly alone before.

She drifted off to sleep a couple times during the night. The morning sun was muted by clouds and fog, creating a gloomy feel. She grabbed her phone and via the hospital's wireless network accessed the internet. She quickly found the number for a rape crisis center. She was about to hit the Send Call button and then paused.

What would she say? *My ex-boyfriend tried to rape and attack me? And oh, by the way, his father runs the biggest hospital in the city and they are protecting him?* For the moment, she put off the call and turned the word over and over again in her mind ... *rape, rape investigation, rape kit.*

She picked up the risk manager's card on her dusty, laminated nightstand, where it had sat near the stained coffee rings. She dialed the extension and got voice mail. She left a message. If they had done a rape exam on her, there would be a rape kit. This could be her salvation.

She now remembered her last night with Josh. He had been drinking heavily as usual. He demanded sex, and at first she agreed until he demanded it be anal. Then she said an emphatic *No.* Although he was not a large man, he worked out in the gym daily and he grabbed her blouse, ripping it off her. He turned her over and pulled up her skirt. She felt the pain and thought she was being ripped apart.

Her doctors said she could be discharged the next day. She could continue with therapy as an outpatient for another month and stay off work for the same amount of time. They were encouraged with her progress and optimistic about a full return of her memory. Before she even went home the next day however, she drove her rusty Toyota Corolla to the Seattle Police Department to ask about the results of her rape test. A large, kind, black woman sat at the computer and squinted at her through the tiny circle cut out of the safety glass divider. After a few minutes of searching, the secretary spoke.

"Oh, I've found it. But I'm sorry, honey, the kit has not been processed yet."

"How is that even possible? My attack was almost one week ago."

"Unfortunately, we have tests that lie around untested for months, even years. I wish I could be more help to you. Do you have a lawyer?"

"Lawyer? No. I don't have much money."

"How about a public defender?"

Alice shook her head. The woman slid a business card under the glass and it had the location and phone number of the public defender's office next door.

"Go see them," she said. "Maybe they can help."

She took the card and started to leave but became overwhelmed. She collapsed on the dark wood bench next to the exit door and began to sob softly. She reached in her purse for a tissue. Her mind, which up until yesterday was a complete fog, began to race with scary and fearful thoughts.

"I live alone. I'm not even sure I should be driving, and I forgot to ask the doctors about that. I have no food in the house and only $50 in my checking account. My cell phone was stolen during the attack. How will I ever work? How will I survive? I might end up on the street." Then it struck her. This is what he wanted all along—to isolate her and force her back to him.

Her amnesia was lifting. She began to think about her

family. And that's when she decided to make the phone call she had been dreading. Her father had died suddenly ten years ago of brain cancer. Her mother had become a born again Christian and never forgave Alice for her failed first marriage to a two-timing, coke-sniffing con artist. They had, in fact, not spoken in years. And she lived on the opposite coast in South Carolina.

Alice reached into her purse and surveyed the sparse contents. The black address book was there and it contained her mother's phone number. She went back to the glass window and tried to cover her sniffles and wipe her damp cheeks.

"I'm sorry to bother you again, but I lost my phone. Could I please borrow one for a collect call?"

The woman pointed across the hall to a payphone—something Alice had not seen in years—and shoved a quarter under the window tray.

After a few rings her mother answered. At first there was hesitation in accepting the call but then she consented.

"Mom, this is Alice. I'm in trouble and I need your help."

The conversation was awkward and it didn't take long before Alice started to cry. Fortunately, her mother was in a forgiving mood and did not lecture her too much about accepting Christ as her savior. She would wire her some money and fly out to help her get back on her feet.

She walked down the street to the public defender's office. A wintry mist hung to the streets and buildings. Everything was damp. A homeless man sat on the steps with his hand outstretched.

"I just had to borrow 25 cents for a phone call so you got the wrong person," she said. He shifted eye contact to the next person.

The inside was cold granite with stone benches and water-stained paint that was peeling off the walls. She approached the glass divider and explained her dilemma to a man in a drab blue uniform.

"We usually don't have same-day appointments," he said.

Her eyes began to tear up again.

"However, let me see if one of the PD staff is free."

"What's PD?"

"Public Defender. That's what you asked for, correct?"

"Yes," she said with her head bowed.

"Wait over there," he said pointing to the granite slab.

She sat down for what seemed liked hours. People came and went and no one said hello or even made eye contact. She had never felt so alone in the world.

Finally, she heard her name called and she approached the window.

"Miriam Jacobs will see you now. Follow the hall to the right. It's the third door on the right." He buzzed her through the wooden swing door. As she walked in, she noted two of three ceiling lights were burnt out, giving the hallway a dank, morose, and almost prison-like atmosphere.

Miriam's door was open. The petite woman waved her in and signaled for her to sit in the wood chair in front of her desk. Miriam had a high-pitched voice that made her look even younger than her size and demeanor suggested. She extended her hand to Alice, who immediately tried to guess her age.

"I know what you're thinking," the counselor said. "Is she really old enough to be a lawyer?"

Alice's face got red and she managed a half smile. "I'm sorry; was it that obvious?"

"No worries. I get it all the time. I bet your next question is, Why would you want to work in the PD office?"

"Actually, no," Alice said. "Why would I wonder that?"

"Because most people do and the pay sucks. Anyway, most of my clients are guilty. It's depressing. But I just finished law school and I need to pay some college and law school loans. I figure if I work here for forty years, I might be able to pay off about half of them."

Alice smiled a little bit more. She liked her already.

"So what brings you here?" Miriam said waving her hand around the gloomy office. There was one desk lamp, no artwork, no photos, and no diplomas on the wall. There was one dried-up Christmas cactus in a terra-cotta pot on the corner of the desk. Its shriveled flowers and leaves appeared to be ready to drop at any second.

After Alice explained her situation, Miriam sat back in her chair and folded her arms across her chest.

"Hmm."

"What?" Alice asked.

"It's just that you haven't been accused of a crime, so I'm the wrong person to be your counsel." Miriam could see Alice's shoulders drop and her lower lip started to tremble.

"However, I do know someone at a local firm who owes me a favor. He might be willing to do some *pro bono* work."

"I assume you don't have any money; otherwise, you wouldn't have been referred here, correct?"

Alice nodded her head.

Miriam picked up her cell phone and punched in some numbers. After a moment, her face became animated and she began to speak.

"Hi Daryl, this is Mir. How are you doing?"

"Yes, me too. No, I don't want to go out for drinks with you again," she said, winking to Alice. "But I do have a favor to ask."

After some back and forth banter, which Alice felt involved a hook-up date in the future, the phone call ended with Miriam saying, "Thanks a bunch. You're the bomb."

She wrote Daryl's name, address, and phone number on the back of one of her plain black and white business cards, and said, "Good luck."

They shook hands. Alice shoved the card into her bra and left the office feeling more hopeful.

She drove home with an almost empty gas tank, literally on fumes, as black storm clouds and some rain began to fall. As she approached her apartment, something didn't feel right. At first she could not identify it, and then she noticed the door had been jimmied open. The wood was cracked and the peeling paint looked freshly picked off. Her heart began to pound. Her mouth dried up as her breathing increased. Pausing for a moment, she didn't know if she should go in or run away. She quickly scanned the stoop and saw one of the neighbor boys had left a Louisville slugger on the top of the stairs. She picked up the bat and pushed the door open about a foot.

There were no lights on inside. The dampness went through her bones and made her shivering even worse. She was only in a few feet when she stepped on something large but squishy. There was just enough light to see through the window and she gasped. Her pet calico cat, Oscar, lay motionless on the carpet, blood streaming out of his nose, mouth, and ears. She wanted to scream but only gripped the bat tighter.

"Hello, Alice," said a familiar voice from the kitchen. He was dressed in all black with a balaclava over his face. "I'm sorry about Oscar, but you never had him declawed. You know he never liked me. Well today, when I came in, he went straight for my leg, and I had to teach him a lesson. You can get another off the street anyway. There's thousands out there."

She stood motionless, with the bat hidden behind her. She was afraid to speak, so she let him ramble on.

"We were so good together. You never should have left me. I just can't see you with anyone else, you know. Can't we give us another try?"

She was afraid to move. Now she remembered the terror and the abuse. She remembered him feeding her Oxycontin pills and wine after he had punched her in the belly. Then she had passed out.

"No, Josh, there is no more *us*. How could you possibly think that after all you've done to me?"

He started towards her slowly and she instinctively began to back up.

"What's that behind your back?" he asked.

"It's nothing," she said, her voice trembling.

"Really? Then if it's nothing, let me see it. As soon as he said that, she saw the handgun dangling by his right side. She had no doubt he would use it. Suddenly, all of her rage from the abusive relationship welled up inside her. If she were going to die, she'd die fighting.

Josh moved closer and was now less than ten feet away. Again, she could smell his hideous cologne.

"Don't come any closer," she warned him, "or I'll ..."

"Or you'll what? Shoot me?" Then he laughed and raised the gun. Before it could reach forty-five degrees from his thigh she lunged. He got off two shots, one of which whizzed through her left earlobe and she felt blood. As the meat of the bat descended onto Josh's left forearm, she heard the crack of bone. He fell backward and screamed. As he raised his right arm to shoot again she reacted quicker. This time the bat came down on his right hand, and she listened as his metacarpals shattered. He dropped to his knees, the black gun falling to the floor. She kicked it away from him.

"You bitch," he slurred. "When I'm done with you, you'll wish you were dead."

He tried to tackle her, leading the way with a vicious head butt. But she was too quick. With a swift backhand, she swung the bat against his skull, and he tumbled to the ground in a heap. The crack of head made a hideous sound. He didn't move at first. She approached him and saw blood streaming out of his ear and cheek. He rolled over like a log and his gaze fixed on the gun. Before he could crawl, however, she let out a scream and the bat came down again and again, smashing his cranium like a melon. Bits of bone and brain splattered everywhere. All of her pent-up anger and frustration burst forth in loud screams. There were several knocks on her door. At first she did not hear them until they became louder. She stood there, paralyzed and unable to move. She felt a hand on her shoulder. She quickly turned and was about to swing the bat.

"Whoa, whoa, whoa. It's me, Sam, your neighbor. I heard shots and ran over. Oh my God. Who is that?" he asked, pointing to the bloodied heap on her carpet.

"My ex-boyfriend. He tried to kill me. Can you call the police?"

Sam could see she was about to faint and caught her in his arms before she hit the floor. As a paramedic, he knew what to do. He grabbed some pillows from the couch and propped her legs up so they were higher than the rest of her body and blood could get to her brain. He covered her with a throw from the sofa and saw her bleeding ear. He took off his shirt and applied pressure to her oozing ear with one hand. With the other one he dialed 911.

At police headquarters, she endured several more hours of interrogation. She was beyond exhausted. The police pumped her full of hot coffee and vending machine snacks as she recounted the events of the day and the past few weeks.

At one point, she asked, "Is he dead?"

The policeman nodded his head.

"Will I be charged and put in jail?"

"I don' think so, but you may want to call your lawyer. Do you have one?"

She thought for a moment and took the card out of her bra. The policeman turned the black clunky phone on the desk toward her and punched in Daryl's phone number. It was almost midnight, but luckily the number she had was his mobile phone.

"Hello," Daryl asked, groggy and half-asleep.

"Uh, this is Alice, I spoke with you earlier today."

"Alice, uh yes. Why are you calling me so late?"

"I just killed someone ... in self-defense."

"Then I think you need to call someone else."

"Who would that be?"

"Alice, seriously? Turn the card over. Now you need a public defender."

Miriam expedited her release from the police and got her off on all charges. They soon became fast friends and went out for coffee, drinks, and dinner often. She also lined her up with a plaintiff's attorney and they filed a multi-million dollar lawsuit against Memorial Hospital on multiple counts including employee abuse, lack of security, and knowingly harboring a criminal. Depositions and negotiations dragged on for months. One week before going to trial, the hospital settled out of court for a million dollars plus five million in punitive damages.

Alice still felt alone and adrift. The dark cloud of abuse hanging over her never seemed to lift. However, she volunteered at a rape crisis center and donated a large portion of her settlement to battered and abused women. She bought and moved to a houseboat on Puget Sound and got a new cat. During the depressing cold and cloudy months, she would think back to her days of nursing and abusive relationships. Anti-depressant medications and therapy helped.

Her mother moved to Seattle to be closer and they spent every day with each other. It was awkward at first, but with time they became close friends. They would shop and go to movies and eat dinners together. They even did touristy thinks like visit the Space Needle and Pike's Market.

When summer finally came, she began to date a man at the rape center. He had been abused as a child as well. However, unlike Josh, he chose to break the cycle and was kind, gentle, and loving to her. The thing she liked best about him was his nickname for her—"Sunshine."

Light & Dark

Acknowledgments

I would like to thank and acknowledge my wife, Denise, for her support and motivation for this work. Also, I would like to express gratitude to many Facebook friends for their suggestions and comments. I also appreciate Joan Greenblatt's help in cover and interior design, as well with book uploading for printing and electronic versions. And finally, thank you to Lynda Lippman-Lockhart for her critical comments and suggestions.